The idea first arose from a discussion after ___ld science fiction convention in London: why not get a ___ber of writers to produce stories on a set theme? The pros ___ cons of the idea were argued far into the night by the contributors to this volume – Brian Aldiss, Poul Anderson, James Blish and Harry Harrison – and Kyril Bonfiglioli, editor of the magazine *Science Fantasy*, later named *Impulse*. Finally an agreement was reached and the first series of stories, on the theme 'sacrifice', appeared in that magazine. The impetus to expand this successful formula into a complete book came from Harry Harrison, and more stories were produced, this time on the balancing theme of 'redemption'.

FOUR FOR THE FUTURE

An Anthology on the themes
of Sacrifice and Redemption

Q _____

EDITED BY HARRY HARRISON

QUARTET BOOKS   LONDON

Published by Quartet Books Limited 1974
27 Goodge Street, London W1P 1FD

First published in Great Britain by
Macdonald & Co (Publishers) Limited 1969

ISBN 0 704 31093 7

Made and printed in Great Britain by
C. Nicholls & Company Ltd
The Philips Park Press, Manchester

for
KYRIL BONFIGLIOLI
who pointed us in the direction and pushed

CONTENTS

INTRODUCTION

It was well past midnight when the idea was first broached, and at first it appeared to have all the hallmarks of the sort of notion that is discussed when the hour is late and the glasses are low. But the more it was considered the more intriguing it became until, finally, it was entertained seriously.

Writers are individualists – or they would not be writers. It has been said, more than once, that if twenty-five writers were given the identical idea, the result would be twenty-five different stories. This has always been assumed to be correct, and seemed so obvious, at least to the writers, that it was never put to the test.

It has been now.

This was in Oxford, in September, a time of clear bright days and crisp nights. There had been a world science fiction convention a few days earlier in London, attended by enthusiasts and writers from all over the world. SF, as it should be, has become international of late, so the Germans were there, the Norwegians, Italians, Yugoslavs and French. And the Americans of course, since modern SF is, for the most part, a British and American creation. The convention, in the manner of these things, was entitled the Loncon. (In New York City it is the Nycon, Chicago the Chicon, San Francisco the Baycon, and so forth.) The writers, some of whom had met their opposite numbers for the first time, gravitated towards Oxford where the talk continued a few days more in a sort of unofficial Oxcon.

That is the scene. The circle is gathered in Brian Aldiss's living room and the hour is late, although no one notices. Drink is to hand and an argument is taking place. All are attacking and a single soul is defending. You must meet him. He is Kyril Bonfiglioli, the then editor of the magazine *Science Fantasy*, soon to change its title to *Impulse*. Editing was just one of his many endeavours, for Mr Bonfiglioli, fellow of Balliol, art collector, art dealer, antiquarian, linguist, Army Sabre Champion, is a man of many parts. Now, cool and aloof, over a beaker of golden šljivovica, he holds the pack at bay.

He does not agree with them. He has his nerve. Mere courtesy demands that, on a point of science fiction, he agree with any argument defended by Brian W. Aldiss, Poul Anderson, James Blish and Harry Harrison. Poppycock, or perhaps something worse, he mutters.

The argument for his opponents seems sound. After all – who should know better? They say, in loud unison, that ideas are personal and concepts must be transmogrified by the writer, filtered through his own personality. An idea is but a mirror for the author's image. Poppycock? Not again.

Slowly, reluctantly, Bonfiglioli is won over. Can he be made to see the light? Brian has a suggestion that will prove the point. He proposes that the authors present shall each write a story on a common theme for *Impulse*, perhaps on 'sacrifice'. Agreed, the others say, but Bon is not so easily convinced. Everything, short of striking the man, is done to convince him of the wisdom of this course. There is a brisk rattle of verbal sabres and victory is close. The writers will produce . . .

What will they produce? Bonfiglioli, cool and inscrutable, touches bottle to glass. The writers are thoughtful, silent. They will prove their point. Each will write a story on the theme of 'sacrifice' and the editor will print all the stories in a special issue of his magazine. Who has won?

Who will get almost an entire issue of his magazine produced for him by some of the top names in the field? Is there the flicker of a fleeting smile on the expressionless Bonfiglioli features?

It is really you, the reader, who has won. Here are the stories, as they were written for *Science Fantasy* – with a bonus. The writers have been put to work once again. 'Sacrifice' is a general human theme with roots that can be traced to animal behaviour. The mother wolf will lead the hunters away from her den and her young – often losing her own life in the process. Let us then consider a theme that is typically human, even typically western in its considerations: Redemption. In the religious sense it is a deliverance from the bondage of sin. Philosophically, it can mean an expiation of guilt or wrong. Driven once more to their typewriters, our authors have considered redemption, and what it can mean in science fiction.

For modern SF acknowledges no boundaries. It is not attempting to engulf and absorb all of modern fiction, as its wildest enthusiasts would have it, but it does range with complete freedom over space and time. And in the human heart. For modern science fiction is most concerned with the impact of science, civilization, art, change – everything – upon the individual. Whereas stone-age SF was satisfied to blast off in a rocket ship, modern SF, if it mentions rockets at all, is more concerned with the reactions of the people inside of them rather than the details of the propulsion system.

Being part of the general field of fiction, science fiction cannot pretend to be of greater interest than the whole. But it can lay claim to awareness: it does not sleepwalk through the contemporary world, eyes shut. Ninety-five per cent of all the scientists who have ever existed, are alive today. Our lives are being made better, worse, happier, duller – are being affected in every way by the impact of science. The science fiction writer knows this, considers the constantly altering situation, and allows it to affect his vision of reality. When this awareness comes through in a story it produces that odd trickle of satisfaction that can only be found in science fiction.

This book is unusual in that, although written around two concrete themes, it has been written by four different authors. I am one of the four, and the work that I have done to assemble this volume has been mostly that of a committee chairman. No one has been told what to do: each has written on these paired themes as he sees fit.

Alas, the magazine *Impulse* is no more, having been slain in its youth by distribution troubles unrelated to its healthy sale. Kyril Bonfiglioli is, we assume, pleasantly occupied with more important matters now. The issue of *Impulse* in which some of these stories first appeared – with its handsome cover by Judith Ann Lawrence, in private life Mrs James Blish – is now mouldering to dust, a collector's item among the knowledgeable. I must admit to a feeling of pride for having rescued these stories from oblivion, and then seeing the basic themes expanded upon. May you, the reader, enjoy them as much as I have.

HARRY HARRISON

Brian W. Aldiss

THE CIRCULATION OF
THE BLOOD...

I

Under the impact of sunlight, the ocean seemed to burn. Out of the confusion of its flames and its long breakers, an old motor vessel was emerging, engine thudding as it headed for the narrow channel among the coral reefs. Two or three pairs of eyes watched it from the shore, one pair protected behind dark glasses from the glare beyond.

The *Kraken* shut off its engines. As it slid between the pincers of coral, it let off a double blast from its siren. Minutes later, it lost all forward momentum, and an anchor rattled down on to the collapsed coral bed, clearly visible under the water. Then it was rubbing its paintless hull against the landing stage.

The landing stage, running out from the shore over the shallow water, creaked and swayed. As it and the ship became one unit, and a negro in a greasy nautical cap jumped down from the deck to secure the mooring lines, a woman detached herself from the shade of the coconut palms that formed a crest to the first rise of the beach.

She came slowly forward, almost cautiously, dangling her sunglasses now from a hand held at shoulder level. She came down on to the landing stage, her sandals creaking and tapping over the slats.

The motor vessel had its faded green canopy up, protecting part of the fore-deck from the annihilating sun. A bearded man stuck his head out of the side of the rail, emerging suddenly from the shadow of the canvas. He wore nothing but a pair of old jeans, rolled high up his calf – jeans, and a pair of steel-rimmed spectacles; his body was tanned brown. He was ambiguously in his mid-forties, a long-faced man called Clement Yale. He was coming home.

Smiling at the woman, he jumped down on to the landing stage. For a moment they stood regarding each other. He looked at the line that now divided her brow, at the slight wrinkles by the corners of her eyes, at the fold that increasingly encompassed her full mouth. He saw that she had applied lipstick and powder for this great event of his return. He was moved by what he saw; she was still beautiful – and in that phrase, 'still beautiful', was the melancholy echo of another thought. She tires, she tires, although her race is not half-run!

'Caterina!' he said.

As they went into each other's arms, he thought, but perhaps, perhaps it could now be arranged that she would live – well, let's be conservative and say . . . say six or seven hundred years . . .

After a minute, they broke apart. The sweat from his torso had marked her dress. He said, 'I must help them unload a few essentials, darling, then I'll be with you. Where's Philip? He's still here, isn't he?'

'He's somewhere around,' she said, making a vague gesture at the backdrop of palms, their house, and the scrub-clad cliff behind that – the only high ground on Kalpeni. She put the sunglasses on again, and Yale turned back to the ship.

She watched him move sparely, recalling that laconic and individual way he had of ordering both his sentences and his limbs. He set about directing the eight crew quietly, joking with Louis, the fat creole cook from Mauritius, supervising the removal of his electron microscope. Gradually a small pile of boxes and trunks appeared on the wooden quay. Once she looked round to see if Philip was about, but the boy was not to be seen.

She moved back to the shore as the men began to shoulder their loads. Without looking round, she climbed the board walk over the sand, and went into the house.

Most of the baggage from the ship was taken into the laboratory next door, or the store adjoining it. Yale brought up the rear, carrying a hutch made from old orange boxes. Between the bars of the hutch, two young Adelie penguins peered, croaking to each other.

He walked into the house by the back door. It was a simple

6

one-storey structure, built of chunks of coral and thatched in the native manner, or the native manner before the Madrassis had started importing corrugated iron to the atolls.

'You'd like a beer, darling,' she said, stroking his arm.

'Can't you rustle up some for the boys? Where's Philip?'

'I said I don't know.'

'He must have heard the ship's siren.'

'I'll get some beer.'

She went through into the kitchen where Joe, the boy, was lounging at the door. Yale looked round the cool familiar living-room, at the paperbacks propped up with seashells, the rug they had bought in Bombay on the way out here, the world map and the oil portrait of Caterina hanging on the walls. It had been months since he had been home – well, it really was home, though it was in fact only a fisheries research station to which they had been posted. Caterina was here, so it must be home, but they could now think about getting back to the U.K. The research stint was over, the tour of duty done. It would be better for Philip if they went home to roost, at least temporarily, while he was still at university. Yale went to the front door and looked along the length of the island.

Kalpeni was shaped like an old-fashioned beer bottle opener, the top bar of which had been broken by sea action to admit small boats into the lagoon. Along the shaft of the island grew palms. Right at the far end lay the tiny native settlement, a few ugly huts, not visible from here because of intervening higher ground.

'Yes, I'm home,' he said to himself. Along with his happiness ran a thread of worry, as he wondered how he'd ever face the gloom of the Northern European climate.

He saw his wife through the window talking to the crew of the trawler, watched their faces and drew pleasure from their pleasure in looking at and talking to a pretty woman again. Joe trotted behind her with a tray full of beers. He went out and joined them, sat on the bench beside them and enjoyed the beer.

When he had the chance, he said to Caterina, 'Let's go and find Philip.'

'You go, darling. I'll stay and talk to the men.'

'Come with me.'

'Philip will turn up. There's no hurry.'

'I've something terribly important to tell you.'

She looked anxious. 'What sort of thing?'

7

'I'll tell you this evening.'

'About Philip?'

'No, of course not. Is anything the matter with Philip?'

'He wants to be a writer.'

Yale laughed. 'It isn't long since he wanted to be a moon pilot, is it? Has he grown very much?'

'He's practically an adult. He's serious about being a writer.'

'How've you been, darling? You haven't been too bored? Where's Fräulein Reise, by the way?'

Caterina retreated behind her dark glasses and looked towards the low horizon. 'She's got bored. She went home. I'll tell you later.' She laughed awkwardly. 'We've got much to tell each other, Clem. How was the Antarctic?'

'Oh, marvellous! You should have been with us, Cat! Here it's a world of coral and sea – there it's ice and sea. You can't imagine it. It's clean. All the time I was there, I was in a state of excitement. It's like Kalpeni – it will always belong to itself, never to man.'

When the crew were moving back to the ship, he put on a pair of canvas shoes and strolled out towards the native huts to look for his son, Philip.

Among the shanties, nothing moved. Just clear of the long breakers, a row of fishing boats lay on the sand. An old woman sat against the elephant-grey bole of a palm, watching an array of jewfish drying before her, too idle to brush the flies away from her eyelids. Nothing stirred but the unending Indian Ocean. Even the cloud over distant Karavatti was anchored there. From the largest hut, which served also as a store, came the thin music of a radio and a woman singing.

> Happiness, oh Happiness,
> It's what you are, it's not Progress.

The same, Yale thought to himself dryly, applied to laziness. These people had the good life here, or their version of it. They wanted to do nothing, and their wish was almost entirely fulfilled. Caterina also liked the life. She could enjoy looking at the vacant horizon day after day. He had always to be doing. You had to accept that people differed – but he had always accepted that, taken pleasure in it.

He ducked his head and went into the big hut. A genial and plump young Madrassi, all oiled and black and shining, sat behind his counter picking his teeth. His name was over the

8

door, painted painfully on a board in English and Sanskrit, 'V. K. Vandranasis'. He rose and shook hands with Yale.

'You are glad to get back from the South Pole, I presume?'

'Pretty glad, Vandranasis.'

'Without doubt the South Pole is cold even in this warm weather?'

'Yes, but we've been on the move, you know – covered practically ten thousand nautical miles. We didn't simply sit on the Pole and freeze! How's life with you? Making your fortune?'

'Now, now, Mr Yale, on Kalpeni are no fortunes to be made. That you surely know!' He beamed with pleasure at Yale's joke. 'But life is not too bad here. Suddenly you know we got a swarm of fish here, more than the men can catch. Kalpeni never before got so many fish!'

'What sort of fish? Jewfish?'

'Yes, yes, many many jewfish. Other fish not so plenty, but the jewfish are now in their millions.'

'And the whales still come?'

'Yes, yes, when it is full moon the big whales are coming.'

'I thought I saw their carcasses up by the old fort.'

'That is perfectly correct. Five carcasses. The last one last month and one the month before at the time of the full moon. I think maybe they come to eat the jewfish.'

'That can't be. The whales started visiting the Laccadives before we had a glut of jewfish. In any case, blue whales don't eat jewfish.'

V. K. Vandranasis put his head cutely on one side and said, 'Many strange things happen you science wallahs and learned men don't know. There's always plenty change happening in the old world, don't you know? Maybe this year the blue whales newly are learning to appreciate eating the jewfish. At least, that is my theory.'

Just to keep the man in business, Yale bought a bottle of raspberryade and drank the warm scarlet liquid as they chatted. The storekeeper was happy to give him the gossip of the island, which had about as much flavour to it as the sugary mess Yale was drinking. In the end, Yale had to cut him short by asking if he had seen Philip; but Philip had not been down this end of the island for a day or two it appeared. Yale thanked him, and started back along the strip of beach, past the old woman still motionless before her drying fish.

9

He wanted to get back and think about the jewfish. The months-long survey of ocean currents he had just completed, which had been backed by the British Ministry of Fisheries and Agriculture and the Smithsonian Oceanic Research Institute under the aegis of the World Waters Organization, had been inspired by a glut of fish – in this case, a super-abundance of herring in the over-fished waters of the Baltic, which had begun ten years ago and continued ever since. That superabundance was spreading slowly to the herring banks of the North Sea; in the last two years, those once-vast reservoirs of fish had been yielding and even surpassing their old abundance. He knew, too, from his Antarctic expedition, that the Adelie penguins were also greatly on the increase. And there would be other creatures, also pro-liferating, unrecorded as yet.

All these apparently random increases in animal population seemed not be have been made at the expense of any other animal – though obviously that state of affairs would not be maintained if the numbers multiplied to really abnormal proportions.

It was a coincidence that these increases came at a time when the human population explosion had tailed off. Indeed, the explosion had been more of a dread myth than an actuality; now it had turned into a phantom of might-have-been, rather like the danger of uncontained nuclear war, which had also vanished in this last decade of the old twentieth century. Man had not been able to voluntarily curtail his reproductive rate to any statistically significant extent, but the mere fact of over-crowding with all its attendant physical discomforts and anti-familial pressures, and with its psychic pressures of neurosis, sexual aberration, and sterility operating exactly in the areas previously most fecund, had proved dynamic enough to level off the accelerating birth spiral in the dense population centres. One result of this was a time of tranquillity in international affairs such as the world had hardly known throughout the rest of the century.

It was curious to think of such matters on Kalpeni. The Laccadives lay awash in ocean and sun; their lazy peoples lived on a diet of dry fish and coconut, exporting nothing but dry fish and copra; they were remote from the grave issues of the century – of any century. And yet, Yale reminded himself, misquoting Donne, no island is an island. Already these shores were lapped by the waves of a new and mysterious change that was flooding the world for better or worse – a change over which man had absolutely no command, any more than he could command the flight of the lonely albatross through the air above the southern oceans.

II

Caterina came out of the coral-built house to meet her husband.

'Phil's home, Clem!' she said, taking his hand.

'Why the anxiety?' he asked, then saw his son emerge from the shade, ducking slightly to avoid the lintel of the door. He came forward and put his hand out to his father. As they shook hands, Philip smiling and blushing, Yale saw he had indeed grown adult.

This son by his first marriage – Yale had married Caterina only three and a half years ago – looked much as Yale himself had done at seventeen, with his fair hair clipped short and a long mobile face that too easily expressed the state of mind of its owner.

'Good to see you again. Come on in and have a beer with me,' Yale said. 'I'm glad the *Kraken* got back here before you had to leave for England.'

'Well, I wanted to speak to you about that, Father. I think I'd better go home on the *Kraken* – I mean, get a lift in it to Aden, and fly home from there.'

'No! They sail tomorrow, Phil! I shall see so little of you. You don't have to leave so soon, surely?'

Philip looked away, then said as he sat down at the table opposite his father, 'Nobody asked you to be away the best part of a year.'

The answer caught Yale unexpectedly. He said, 'Don't think I haven't missed you and Cat.'

'That doesn't answer the question, does it?'

'Phil, you didn't ask me a question. I'm sorry I was away so long, but the job had to be done. I hoped you'd be able to stay here a bit longer, so that we could see more of each other. Why have you got to go all of a sudden?'

The boy took the beer that Caterina had brought, raised his glass to her as she sat down between them, and took a long drink. Then he said, 'I have to work, Father. I take finals next year.'

'You're going to stay with your mother in the U.K.?'

'She's in Cannes or somewhere with one of her rich boyfriends. I'm going to stay in Oxford with a friend and study.'

11

'A girl friend, Phil?'

The attempt at teasing did not come off. He repeated sullenly, 'A friend.'

Silence overcame them. Caterina saw they were both looking at her neat brown hands, which lay before her on the table. She drew them on to her lap and said, 'Well, let's all three of us go and have a swim in the lagoon, the way we used to.'

The two men rose, but without enthusiasm, not liking to refuse.

They changed into their swim things. Excitement and pleasure buoyed Yale as he saw his wife in a bikini again. Her body was as attractive as ever, and browner, her thighs not an ounce too heavy, her breasts firm. She grinned naughtily at him as if guessing his thoughts and took his hand in hers. As they went down to the landing stage, carrying flippers and goggles and snorkels, Yale said, 'Where were you hiding out when the *Kraken* arrived, Phil?'

'I was in the fort, and I was not hiding.'

'I was only asking. Cat says you're taking up writing?'

'Oh, does she?'

'What are you writing? Fiction? Poetry?'

'I suppose you'd call it fiction.'

'What would you call it?'

'Oh, for Christ's sake, stop examining me, can't you? I'm not a bloody kid any more, you know!'

'Sounds as if I came back on the wong day!'

'Yes, you did, if you want to know! You divorced Mother and then you went chasing after Cat and married her – why don't you look after her if you want her?'

He flung his equipment down, took a run along the wooden platform, and made a fast shallow dive into the blue waters. Yale looked at Caterina, but she avoided his stare.

'He sounds as if he's jealous! Have you been getting a lot of this sort of thing?'

'He's at the moody stage. You must leave him alone. Don't annoy him.'

'I've hardly spoken to him.'

'Don't oppose his going away tomorrow if he's set on it.'

'You two have been quarrelling over something, haven't you?'

He was looking down at her. She was sitting on the platform, putting on her flippers. As he looked down at the well between her breasts, love overcame him again. They must go back to

12

London, and Cat must start a baby, for her sake; you could sacrifice too much just for the sake of sunlight; civilized behaviour could be defined as a readiness to submit to increased doses of artificial light and heat; maybe there was a direct relationship between the ever-growing world demand for power and a bolstering of the social contract. His moment's speculation was checked by her reply.

'On the contrary, we got on very well when you weren't here.'

Something in her tone made him stand where he was, looking after her as she swam towards her stepson, sporting in the middle of the lagoon beyond the *Kraken*. Slowly, he pulled down his goggles and launched himself after her.

The swim did them all good. After what Vandranasis had said, Yale was not surprised to find jewfish in the lagoon, although they generally stayed on the outer side of the atoll. There was one fat old fellow in particular, over six feet long and half-inclined to set up a leering and contemptuous friendship that made Yale wish he had brought the harpoon gun.

When he had had enough, Yale swam over to the north-west side of the lagoon, below the old Portuguese fort, and lay in the gritty coral sand. The others came and joined him in a few minutes.

'This is the life,' he said, putting an arm round Caterina. 'Some of our so-called experts explain all of life in terms of our power drives, others see everything explicable in terms of God's purpose; for another, it's all a matter of glands, or for another it boils down to a question of sublimated incest-wishes. But for me, I see life as a quest for sunlight.'

He caught his wife's strained look.

'What's the matter? Don't you agree?'

'I – no, Clem, I – well, I suppose I have other goals.'

'What?'

When she didn't answer, he said to Philip, 'What are your goals in life, young man?'

'Why do you ask such boring questions? I just live. I don't intellectualize all the time.'

'Why did Fräulein Reise go home? Was it because you were as discourteous to her as you are to me?'

'Oh, go to . . .' He got up, roughly pulled on his mask, and flung himself back in the water, striking out violently for the far beach. Yale stood up, kicked off his flippers, and trod up beach, ignoring the sharp bite of the coral sand. Over the top of

13

the bank, scraggy grass grew, and then the slope tilted down towards the reef and the long barrier of ocean. Here the whales lay rotting, half out of water, flesh that was now something too terrible to count any more as flesh. Fortunately the south-west trades kept the stench away from the other side of the island; sniffing it now, Yale recalled that this scent of corruption had trailed far across the sea to the *Kraken*, as if all Kalpeni were the throne of some awful and immeasurable crime. He thought of that now, as he tried to control his anger against his son.

That evening, they gave supper to the men of the little trawler. It was a genial farewell meal, but it broke up early and afterwards Yale, Philip and Caterina sat on the veranda, taking a final drink and looking across to the lights of the *Kraken* in the lagoon. Philip seemed to have completely recovered from his earlier sulkiness and was taking cheerfully, burbling on about life at the university until finally Caterina interrupted him.

'I've heard enough about Oxford over the past few weeks. How about hearing about the Antarctic from Clem?'

'It all sounds a gloomy dump to me.'

'It has its vile moments and its good moments,' Clem said, 'which I suppose could be claimed for Oxford too. Take these penguins I've brought back. The conditions in which their species mate are death to man – perhaps minus thirty degrees fahrenheit and with a howling snowstorm moving over them at something like eighty miles an hour. You'd literally freeze solid in that sort of weather, yet the penguins regard it as ideal for courting.'

'More fool them!'

'They have their reasons. At certain times of the year, Antarctica is swimming with food, the richest place in the world. Oh, you'll have to go there one day, Philip. Great doses of daylight in the summer! It's – well, it's another planet down there, and far more undiscovered than the moon. Do you realize that more people have set foot on the moon than have ever ventured into the Antarctic?'

The reasons for the *Kraken*'s sailing into those far south waters had been purely scientific. The newly established World Water Organization, with its headquarters in a glittering new sky-scraper on the Bay of Naples, had inaugurated a five-year study of oceans, and the rusty old *Kraken* was an inglorious part of the Anglo-American contribution. Equipped with Davis-Swallows and other modern oceanographic instrumentation, it had been

14

at work for many months charting the currents of the Atlantic. During that time, Clement Yale had done an unexpected piece of detective work.

'I told you this morning I had something important to say. I'd better get it off my chest now. You know what a copepod is, Cat?'

'I've heard you speak of them. They're fish, aren't they?'

'They're crustaceans living among the plankton, and a vital link in the food chain of oceans. It's been computed that there may be more individual copepods than there are individuals in all other multi-celled animal classes combined – all human beings, fish, oysters, monkeys, dogs, and so on – the lot. A copepod is about the size of a rice grain. Some genera eat half their own weight in food – mainly diatoms – in a day. The world champion pig never managed that. The rate at which this little sliver of life ingests and reproduces might well stand as a symbol of the fecundity of old Earth.

'It might stand, too, for the way in which all life is linked all round the globe. The copepods feed on the smallest living particles in the ocean, and are eaten by some of the largest, in particular the whale shark and the basking shark and various whales. Several sea-going birds like a bit of copepod in their diet too.

'The different genera of copepods infest different lanes and levels in the multi-dimensional world of the ocean. We followed one genus for thousands of miles while we were tracking one particular ocean current.'

'Oh-oh, I thought he was edging on to his favourite topic!' Philip said.

'Get your father another drink and don't cheek him. The complex of ocean flow is as necessary to human life as the circulation of the blood. The one as much as the other is the stream of existence, bearing us all forward willy-nilly. On the *Kraken* we were interested in one part of that stream in particular, a current of whose existence oceanographers were aware in theory for some time. Now we have charted it exactly, and named it.

'I'll tell you the name of this current in a minute. It'll amuse you, Cat. The current starts lazily in the Tyrrhenian Sea, which is the name of the bit of the Mediterranean between Sardinia, Sicily and Italy. We've swum in it more than once off Sorento, Cat, but to us it was just the "Med". Anyhow, the evaporation rate is higher there, and the extra salty water sinks and spills

15

out eventually into the Atlantic, of which the Med is just a land-locked arm.

'The current sinks further and deflects south. We could follow it quite easily with salinity gauges and flow-rate recorders and so on. It divides, but the particular stream we were interested in remains remarkably homogeneous and comprises a narrow ribbon of water moving at a rate of about three miles a day. In the Atlantic, it is sandwiched between two other currents moving in the opposite direction, currents that have been known for some years as the Antarctic Intermediate Water and the Antarctic Bottom Water. Both these north-flowing streams are considerable masses of water – main arteries, you could call them. The Bottom Water is highly saline and icy cold.

'We followed our current right across the Equator and down into southern latitudes, into the cold waters of the Southern Ocean. It is eventually forced to the surface, fanning out as it rises, from the Weddell to the Mackenzie Sea, along the Antarctic coast. In this warmer water, during the short polar summer, the copepods and other small fry proliferate. Another little crustacean, the euphaustids or "krill", turn the seas cinnamon, so many of them pack the waters. The *Kraken* often rode on a pink sea. While they're feeding on diatoms, the whales are feeding on them.'

'Nature's so horrible!' Caterina said.

Yale smiled at her. 'Maybe, but there's nothing else *but* nature! Anyhow, we were very proud of our current for making such a long journey. Do you know what we have called it? We've named it in honour of the Director of the World Waters Organization. It is to be known as the Devlin Current, after Theodore Devlin, the great marine ecologist and your first husband.'

Caterina looked most striking when she was angry. Reaching for a cigarette from the sandalwood box on the table, she said, 'I suppose that is your idea of a joke!'

'It's an irony perhaps. But it's only fitting, don't you know. Give the devil his due! Devlin's a great man, more important than I shall ever be.'

'Clem, you know how he treated me!'

'Of course I do. Because of that treatment, I was lucky enough to get you. I hold no malice for the man. After all, he was once a friend of mine.'

'No, he wasn't. Theo has no friends, only expediencies. After my five years with him I should know him better than you.'

16

'You could be prejudiced.' He smiled, rather enjoying her annoyance.

She threw the cigarette at him and jumped up. 'You're crazy, Clem! You drive me mad! Why don't you sometimes get your back up at someone? You're always so damned level-tempered. Why can't you hate someone, ever? Theo in particular! Why couldn't you hate Theo for my sake?'

He stood up too. 'I love you when you're trying to be a bitch.'

She smacked him across the face, sending his spectacles flying, and stamped out of the room. Philip did not move. Yale went over to the nearest cane chair and picked his spectacles up from the seat; they were not broken. As he put them on again, he said, 'I hope these scenes don't embarrass you too much, Phil. We all need safety valves for our emotions, women in particular. Caterina's marvellous, isn't she? Don't you think? You did get on well with her, didn't you?'

Philip flushed a slow red. 'I'll leave you to your capers. I have to go and pack.'

As he turned, Yale caught his arm. 'You don't have to go. You are almost adult. You must face violent emotions. You never could as a child – but they're as natural as storms at sea.'

'Child! You're the child, Father! You think you're so poised and understanding, don't you? But you've never understood how people feel!'

He pulled himself away. Yale was left standing in the room alone. '*Explain* and I'd understand,' he said aloud.

III

When he walked into the bedroom, Caterina was sitting dejectedly on her bed, barefoot, with her feet resting on the stone floor. She looked up at him intently, with something of the inscrutable stare of a cat.

'I drank too much tonight, darling. You know beer doesn't agree with me. I'm sorry!'

Yale went over to her, pulled the rug under her feet, and knelt beside her. 'You horrible alcoholic! Come and help me feed the penguins before we turn in. Philip's gone to bed, I think.'

'Say you've forgiven me.'

'Oh, Christ, let's not have *that*, my sweet Cat! You can see I have forgiven you.'

'Say it then, say it!'

He thought to himself, 'Phil's entirely right, I don't understand anyone. I don't even understand myself. It's true I have forgiven Cat; why then should I be reluctant to say so because she insists I say so? Maybe it was because I thought there was so little to forgive. Well, what's a man's dignity beside a woman's need?' And he said it.

Outside, the waves made slumberous noises along the reef, a sound of continuous content. The island looked so low by night that it seemed a wonder the sea did not sweep over it. Not a light showed anywhere except for the lamp on the *Kraken*'s mast.

The two penguins were in one of the permanent cages at the rear of the lab. They stood with their beaks tucked under their flippers, asleep, and did not alter their position when the lights came on.

She put an arm round his waist. 'Sorry I flew off the handle. I suppose we ought to have congratulated you? I mean, I suppose this current is rather a big discovery, isn't it?'

'It's certainly a *long* discovery – nine and a half thousand miles long.'

'Oh, be serious, darling. You're underplaying what you've done as usual, aren't you?'

'Oh, terribly! I may get a knighthood any day. Anyhow, we'll have to fly to London in a week to receive some sort of applause, and I'll have to make a fuller report than I have done so far. In fact there is another discovery that I've only communicated to one other person as yet which makes the discovery of Devlin's Current seem nothing, a discovery that could affect every one of us.'

'What do you mean?'

'It's late and we're both tired. You shall hear about it in the morning.'

'Can't you tell me now, while you're feeding the birds?'

'They're okay. I just wanted to check on them. They'll feed better in the morning.' He looked speculatively at her.

'I am a greedy man, Cat, though I try to hide it. I want life. I'd like to share life with you for a thousand years. I'd like to roam the Earth for a thousand years – with or without a knighthood! That may be possible.'

They stood looking at each other, feeling for the neutral currents that flowed between them, relaxed enough after their tiff to feel that they were no longer two entirely separate organisms.

'There's a new infection in the world's bloodstream,' he said. 'It could bring a sort of illness that we could call longevity. It was first isolated in the herring schools in the Baltic a decade ago. It's a virus, Cat – you understand how we traced the Devlin Current, don't you? We had deep trawls and sonar devices and special floats that sink to predetermined water densities, so that we could trace the particular salinity and temperature and speed of our current all the way. We could also check the plankton content. We found that the copepods carried a particular virus that I could identify as a form of the Baltic virus – it's a highly characteristic form. We don't know where the virus came from originally. The Russians think it was brought to Earth encased in a taktite, or by meteoritic dust, so that it may be extra terrestrial in origin –'

'Clem, please, all this is beyond me! What does this virus *do*? It lengthens life, you say?'

'In certain cases, In certain genera.'

'In men and women?'

'No. Not yet. Not as far as I know.' He gestured towards the equipment on the lab bench. 'I'll show you what it looks like when I get the electron microscope set up. The virus is very small, about twenty millimicrons long. Once it finds a host it can use, it spreads rapidly through the cell tissue, where its action appears to be the destruction of anythino threatening the life of the cell. In fact, it is a cell repairer, and a very effective one at that. You see what that means! Any life form infected with it is inclined to live for ever. The Baltic virus will even re-build cells completely where it finds a really suitable host. So far, it seems to have found only two such hosts, both sea-going, one fish, one mammal, the herring and the blue whale. In the copepods it is merely latent.'

He could see that Caterina was trembling. She said, 'You mean that all herrings and blue whales are – immortal?'

'Potentially so, if they've caught the infection, yes. Of course, the herrings get eaten, but the ones that don't go on reproducing year after year with unimpaired powers. None of the animals that eat the herring appear to catch the infection. In other words, the virus cannot sustain itself in them. It's an irony that this minute germ holds the secret of eternal life, yet is itself threatened constantly with extinction.'

'But people –'

'People don't come into it yet. The copepods we traced along

19

our current were infected with the Baltic virus. They surfaced in the Antarctic. That was one of the discoveries that I made - that there is another species that can be infected. The Adelie penguins have it too. They just don't die from natural causes any more. These two birds here are virtually immortal.'

She stood looking at them through the mesh of the cage. The penguins perched on the edge of their tank, their comical feet gripping its tiled lip. They had awakened without removing their beaks from under their wings, and now regarded the woman with bright and unwinking eyes.

'Clem – it's funny, generations of men have dreamed of immortality. But they never thought it would come to penguins... I suppose that's what you'd call an irony! Is there any way we can infect ourselves from these birds?'

He laughed. 'It's not as easy as picking up psittacosis from a parrot. But it may be that laboratory research will find a means of infecting human beings with this disease. Before that happens, there's another question we ought to ask ourselves.'

'How do you mean?'

'Isn't there a moral question first? Are we capable, either as a species or as individuals, of living fruitfully for a thousand years? Do we deserve it?'

'Do you think herrings deserve it more than we do?'

'They cause less damage than man.'

'Try telling that to your copepods!'

This time he laughed with genuine pleasure, enjoying one of the rare occasions when he considered she answered him back wittily.

'It's interesting the way copepods carry the virus in a latent form all the way down from the Med to the Antarctic without becoming infected themselves. Of course, there must be a connecting link between the Baltic and the Med, but we haven't found it yet.'

'Could it be another current?'

'Don't think so. We just don't know. Meanwhile, the ecology of Earth is slowly being turned upside down. Up till now, it has just meant a pleasant glut of food and the survival of whales that were on the threshold of extinction, but it may lead in time to famines and other unpleasant natural upheavals.'

Caterina was less interested in that aspect. 'Meanwhile, you are going to see if the virus can be implanted in us?'

'That could be very dangerous. Besides, it's not my field.'

'You're not just going to let it slide?'

'No. I've kept the whole matter secret, even from the others on the *Kraken*. I've communicated the problem to only one other person. You'll hate me for this, Cat, but this thing is far too important to let personalities enter the situation. I sent a coded report to Theo Devlin at the WWO in Naples. I shall drop in to see him on our way back to London.'

Suddenly her face looked tired and aged. 'You're either a saint or you're raving mad,' she said.

The penguins watched without moving as the two humans left the room. Long after the lights went out, they shut their eyes and returned to sleep.

Dawn next morning set the sky afire with a more than Wagnerian splendour, revealing the first sluggish activity on the *Kraken*, and mingling with the smell of preserved eggs frying in the galley. In four or five days, the crew would be back at their base in Aden, enjoying fresh and varied food again.

Philip was also astir early. He had slept naked between the sheets and did nothing more in the way of dressing than slipping on a pair of swimming trunks. He walked round the back of the house and looked into his father's bedroom window. Yale and Cat both slumbered peacefully together in her bed. He turned away, his face distorted, and made his way falteringly down to the lagoon for a last swim. A short while later, Joe, the negrito house boy, was bustling round the house, getting the breakfast and singing a song about the coolness of the hour.

As the day grew hotter, the bustle of preparation for departure increased. Yale and his wife were invited aboard the trawler for a farewell lunch, which was eaten under the deck canopy. Although Yale tried to talk to Philip, his son had retired behind his morose mood and would not be drawn; Yale comforted himself by reflecting that they would meet again in the U.K. in a very few days.

The ship sailed shortly after noon, sounding its siren when it moved through the narrow mouth of the reef as it had done when it entered. Yale and Cat waved for a while from the shade of the palms, and then turned away.

'Poor Philip! I hope his holiday did him good. That troubled adolescent phase is hard to deal with. I went through just the same thing, I remember!'

'Did you, Clem? I doubt it.' She looked about her desperately,

21

at her husband's gentle face, at the harsh sea on which the trawler was still clearly visible, up at the heavy leaves of palm above them. In none of these elements, it seemed, could she find help. She burst out, 'Clem, I can't keep it a secret, I must tell you now, I don't know what you'll say or what it'll do to you, but, these last few weeks, Philip and I have been lovers!'

He looked at her in a puzzled way, eyes narrow behind his lenses, as if he could not understand the expression she had used.

'That's why he went off the way he did! He couldn't bear to be around when you were. He begged me never to tell you . . . He . . . Clem, it was all my fault, I should have known better.' She paused and then said, 'I'm old enough to be his mother.'

Yale stood very still, and expelled one long noisy gasp of breath.

'You – you couldn't, Caterina! He's only a boy!'

'He's as adult as you are!'

'He's a boy! You seduced him!'

'Clem, try to see. It was the fräulein originally. She did it to him – or he started it. I don't know which way it was. But it's a small island. I came on them one afternoon, both naked, inside the old fort. I sent her away but somehow the poison spread. I . . . After I'd seen him . . .'

'Oh, God, it's incest!'

'You use these stupid old-fashioned terms!'

'You cow! How could you do it with him?' He turned away. He started walking. She did not stop him. She could not stand still herself. Swinging about in misery, she burst weeping into the house and flung herself on to her unmade bed.

For three hours, Yale stood on the north-west edge of the island, staring paralysed into the sea. In that time, he hardly moved, except once to unhook his spectacles and wipe his eyes. His heart laboured and he glared out at the immensity before him as if challenging it.

She came up quietly behind him, bringing him a glass of water in which she had dissolved lemon crystals.

He took the glass, thanked her quietly, and drank its contents, all without looking at her.

'If it makes any difference, Clement, I love and admire you very much. I'm not fit to be your wife, I know, and I think you are a saint. Much as I hurt you, your hurt was all for what I might have done to Philip, wasn't it?'

'Don't be silly! I shouldn't have left you all these months. I exposed you to temptation.' He looked at her, his face stern. 'I'm sorry for what I said – about incest. You are not related to Philip, except by marriage. In any case, man is the only creature that puts a ban on incest. Most other creatures, including the higher apes, find no harm in it. You can define man as the species that fears incest. Some psycho-analysts define all mental illness as incest-obsessions, you know. So I'm – '

'Stop!' It was almost a scream. For a moment she fought with herself, then she said, 'Look, Clem, talk about *us*, for God's sake, not about what the psycho-analysts say or what the higher apes do! Talk about *us*! Think about *us*!'

'I'm sorry, I'm a pedant, I know, but what I meant – '

'And don't, don't, don't apologize to me! I should be apologizing to you, kneeling, begging for forgiveness! Oh, I feel so awful, so guilty, so desperate! You have no idea what I've been through!'

He seized her painfully and held her, looking for the moment very like his son. 'You're getting hysterical! I don't want you kneeling to me, Cat, though thank heavens it has always been one of your dearest traits that you acknowledge your errors in a way I can never manage with mine. You can see what you've done was wrong. I've thought it all over, and I can see the fault was largely mine. I shouldn't have left you isolated here on Kalpeni for so long. This won't make any difference between us, once I've got over the shock. I've thought it over and I think I just write to Philip and tell him that you've told me everything, and that he is not to feel guilty.'

'Clem – how can you – have you no feeling? How can you have forgiven me so easily?'

'I didn't say I'd forgiven you.'

'You just said it!'

'No, I said – let's not quibble over words. I must forgive you. I have forgiven you.'

She clung to him. 'Then tell me you've forgiven me!'

'I just did.'

'Tell me! Please tell me!'

In a sudden fury, he flung her away from him, crying, 'Damn and blast you, I tell you I have forgiven you, you crazy slut! Why go on?' She fell, sprawling in the sand. Penitently, he stooped to help her up, apologizing for his violence, saying over and over that he had forgiven her. When she was on her feet, they made their way back to the coral-built house, leaving an

23

empty glass lying in the sand. As they went, Caterina said, 'Can you imagine the pain of having to live for a thousand years?'

It was the day after she asked that question that Theodore Devlin arrived on the island.

IV

Almost the entire population of Kalpeni turned out to see the helicopter land on the round chopperport in the centre of the island. Even Vandranasis closed down his little store and followed the thin trickle of spectators northwards.

The great palm leaves clapped together as the machine descended, its WWO insignia gleaming on its black hull. As the blades stopped rotating, Devlin jumped down, followed by his pilot.

Devlin was two or three years Yale's senior, a stocky man in his late forties, well-preserved, and as trim in his appearance as Yale was straggling and untidy. He was a man sharp of face and brain, respected by many, loved by few. Yale, who was wearing nothing but jeans and canvas shoes, strolled over and shook hands with him.

'Fancy seeing you here, Theo! Kalpeni is honoured.'

'Kalpeni is bloody hot! For God's sake, get me in the shade, Clement, before I fry. How you stick it here, I don't know!'

'Gone native, I guess. It's a home from home for me. See n two penguins swimming in the lagoon?'

'Uh.' Devlin was in no mood for small talk. He walk briskly along in a neat light suit, a head shorter than Yale, muscular movements tight and controlled even over the s ing sand.

At the door of his house, Yale stood aside to let his guest the pilot, a lanky Indian, enter. Caterina stood inside the roo her face unsmiling. If Devlin was embarrassed at meeting h ex-wife, he gave no sign of it.

'I thought Naples got hot enough. You're living in a damned oven here. How are you, Caterina? You look well. Haven't seen you since you were weeping in the witness box. How does Clement treat you? Not in the style to which you were once accustomed, I hope?'

'You've obviously not come to make yourself pleasant, Theo. Perhaps you and your pilot would care for a drink. Perhaps you were going to introduce him to us?'

24

After this initial shot across his bows, Devlin pursed his mouth and behaved less pugnaciously. His next remark might even have been construed as an apology. 'Those natives out there annoy me, plastering their fingerprints all over the 'copter. They haven't taken one elementary step forward since mankind began. They're parasites in every sense of the word! They owe their little all to the fish and the wonderful coconut, both brought to their doorstep by the courtesy of the tides – even their damned island was built for them by countless coral insects!'

'Our culture owes the same sort of debt to other plants and animals, and to the earthworm.'

'At least we pay our debts. However, that's neither here nor there. I just don't share your sentimental attachment to desert islands.'

'We didn't invite you to come here, Theo,' Caterina said. She was still suppressing surprise and anger at seeing him.

Joe appeared and served beer to them all. The pilot stood by the open door to drink his, nervously watching his boss. Devlin, Yale, and Caterina sat down facing each other.

'I gather you got my report?' Yale said. 'That's why you're here, isn't it?'

'You're blackmailing me. Thomas!' Devlin snapped his fingers as he spoke, and his pilot produced a pistol fitted with what Yale recognized as a silencer; it was the first time he had ever seen one in real life. The pilot stood holding his beer glass in his left hand, sipping casually, but his glance was far from casual. Yale stood up.

'Sit down!' Devlin said, pointing at him. 'Sit down and listen to me, or it will appear later that you had a misunderstanding with a shark while out swimming. You're up against a tough organization, Clement, but you may come to no harm if you behave. What are you after?'

Yale shook his head. 'You're in trouble, Theo, not I. You'd better explain this whole situation.'

'You're always so innocent, aren't you? I'm well aware that that report you sent me, with your assurance that you had let nobody else know the facts, was a thinly camouflaged piece of blackmail. Tell me how I buy your silence.'

Yale looked at his wife; he read in her face the same bafflement he himself felt. Anger with himself grew in him to think that he could not understand Devlin. What was the fellow after? His report had been merely a scientific summary of the cycle by which the Baltic virus had been carried from the Tyrrhenian Sea down to the Antarctic. Dumbly, he shook his head and dropped his eyes to his folded hands. 'I'm sorry, Theo; you know how terribly naïve I am. I just don't get what you are talking about, or why you should think it necessary to point a gun at us.'

'This is more of your paranoia, Theo!' Caterina said. She got up and walked towards Thomas with her hand out. He put the beer down hastily and levelled the pistol at her. 'Give it to me!' she said. He faltered, his gaze evaded her, she seized the weapon by the barrel, took it from him, and flung it down in one corner of the room.

'Now get out! Go and wait in your helicopter! Take your beer!'

Devlin made a move towards the gun, then stopped. He sat down again, obviously nonplussed. Choosing to ignore Caterina as the only way of saving his dignity, he said, 'Clement, are you serious? You really are such a fool that you don't know what I'm talking about?'

Caterina tapped him on the shoulder. 'You'd better go home. We don't like people to threaten us on this island.'

'Leave him, Kat, let's get out of him whatever extraordinary idea he is nur . . . He comes here all the way from Naples, risking his reput . . . in order to threaten us as if he were a common crook. . . .'

Words failed him.

'What do you want, Ned . . . It's some horrible thing about me, isn't it?'

That restored his humour . . . some of his confidence. 'No, Caterina, it's not! It's noth . . . all to do with you. I lost all interest in you a long, long time . . . long before you ran off with this fisherman!' He got up and crossed to the map of the world hanging dark and fly-spotted, on the wall.

'Clement, you'd better come and look at this. Here's the Baltic. Here's the Med. You tracked the immortality virus all the way from the Baltic right down to the Antarctic. I thought you'd had the wit to grasp how the missing link between the Baltic and Mediterranean was forged; I assumed you were suggesting that your silence could be bought on that score. I over-estimated you! You still haven't got it, have you?'

Yale frowned and stroked his face. 'Don't be so superior, Theo. That area was right beyond my bailiwick. I only started in the Tyrrhenian Sea. Of course, if you know what the link is,

I'd be tremendously interested . . . Presumably it's brought from one sea to the other by a pelagic species. A bird seems a likely agent, but as far as I know nobody has established that the Baltic virus – the immortality virus, you call it – can survive in the body of a bird . . . except the Adelie penguin, of course, but there are none of those in the northern hemisphere.'

Taking his arm, Caterina said, 'Darling, he's laughing at you!'

'Ha, Clement, you are a true man of science! Never see what's under your nose because you're sunk up to your eyes in your own pet theories! You gangling fathead! The vital agent was human – me! I worked on that virus on a ship in the Baltic, I took it back with me to Naples to WWO. H.Q. I worked on it in my own private laboratory, I – '

'I don't see how I was supposed to know – Oh! . . . Theo, you've found it – you've found a way to infect human beings with the virus!'

The expression on Devlin's face was enough to confirm the truth of that. Yale turned to Caterina. 'Darling, you're right and he's right. I really am a short-sighted idiot! I should have guessed. After all, Naples is situated on the Tyrrhenian Sea – it's just that one never thinks of the term and speaks of it always as the Med.'

'You got there at last!' Devlin said. 'That's how the virus leaked into your Devlin Current. There is a small colony of us in Naples with the virus in our veins. It passes out through the body in inert form, and survives the sewage processing, so that it is carried out to sea still living – to be digested by the copepods, as you managed to discover.'

'The circulation of the blood!'

'What?'

'No matter. A metaphor.'

'Theo – Theo, so you are now . . . you have it, do you?'

'Don't be afraid to say it, woman. Yes, I have immortality flowing in my veins.'

Tugging at his beard, Yale went and sat down and took a long drink at his beer. He looked from one to the other of them for a long while. At last he said, 'You are something of the true man of science yourself, Theo, aren't you, as well as a career man? You couldn't resist telling us what you know! But leaving that aside, we of course realized that an inoculation of man with the virus was theoretically possible. Cat and I were discussing it until late last night. Do you know what we decided? We decided that even if it were possible to acquire immortality, or shall we say longevity, we should refuse it. We should refuse it because neither of us feels mature enough to bear the responsibility of our emotional and sexual lives for a span of maybe several hundred years.'

'That's pretty negative, isn't it?' Devlin strolled over to the far corner and retrieved the pistol. Before he could slip it into his pocket, Yale stretched out his hand. 'Until you leave, I'll keep it for you. What were you planning to do with it, anyway?'

'I ought to shoot you, Yale.'

'Give it to me! Then you won't be exposed to temptation. You want to keep your little secret, don't you? How long do you think it will be before it becomes public property anyhow? A thing like that can't be kept quiet indefinitely.'

He showed no sign of giving up the gun. He said, 'We've kept our secret for five years. There are fifty of us now, fifty-three, men with power and some women. Before the secret comes into the open, we are going to be even more powerful: an Establishment. We only need a few years. Meanwhile, we make investments and alliances. Take a look at the way brilliant people have been attracted to Naples these last few years! It's not been just to the WWO. or the European Government Centre. It's been to my clinic! In another five years, we'll be able to step in and rule Europe – and from there it's just a short step to America and Africa.'

'You see,' Caterina said, 'he is mad, Clem, that sort of sane madness I told you about. But he daren't shoot! He daren't shoot, in case they locked him up for life – and that's a long time for him!'

Recognizing the wild note in his wife's voice, Yale told her to sit down and drink another beer. 'I'm going to take Theo round to see the whales. Come on, Theo! I want to show you what you're up against, with all your fruitless ambitions.'

Theo gave him a sharp look, as if speculating whether he might yield useful information if humoured, evidently concluded that he would and rose to follow Yale. As he went out, he looked back towards Caterina. She avoided his glance.

It was dazzling to be out in the bright sun again. The crowd was still hanging about the helicopter, chatting intermittently with the pilot, Thomas. Ignoring them, Yale led Devlin past the machine and round the lagoon, blinding in the glare of noon. Devlin gritted his teeth and said nothing. He seemed diminished as they exposed themselves to a lansdcape almost as bare as an old bone, walking the narrow line between endless blue ocean and the green socket of lagoon.

Without pausing, Yale led on to the north-west strip of beach. It sloped steeply, so that they could see nothing of the rest of the island except the old Portuguese fort, which terminated their view ahead. Grim, black, and ruinous, it might have been some meaningless tumescence erupted by marine forces. As the men tramped towards it, the fort was dwarfed by the intervening carcasses of whales.

Five whales had died here, two of them recently. The giant bodies of the two recently dead still supported rotting flesh, though the skulls gleamed white where the islanders had stripped them for meat and cut out their tongues. The other three had evidently been cast up here at an earlier date, for they were no more than arching skeletons with here and there a fragment of parched skin flapping between rib bones like a curtain in the breeze.

'What have you brought me here for?' Theo was panting, his solid chest heaving.

'To teach you humility and to make you sweat. Look on these works, ye mighty, and despair! These were blue whales, Theo, the largest mammal ever to inhabit this planet! Look at this skeleton! This chap weighed over a hundred tons for sure. He's about eighty feet long.' As he spoke, he stepped into the huge rib cage, which creaked like an old tree as he braced himself momentarily against it. 'A heart beat right here, Theo, that weighed about eight hundredweight.'

'You could have delivered Fifty Amazing Facts of Natural History, or whatever you call this lecture, in the shade.'

'Ah, but this isn't natural history, Theo. It's highly *un*natural. These five beasts rotting here once swallowed krill far away in Antarctic waters. They must have gulped down a few mouthfuls of copepod at the same time – copepods that had picked up the Baltic virus. The virus infected the whales. By your admission, that can only have been five years ago, eh? Yet it is long enough to ensure that more blue whales – they were practically extinct from over-fishing as you know – survived the hazards of immaturity and bred. It would mean too that the breeding period of older specimens was extended. Yet five years is not enough to produce a glut in whales as it is in herrings.'

'What are blue whales doing near the Laccadives in any case?'

'I never found a way to ask them. I only know that these creatures appeared off shore here at full moon, each in a different month. Caterina could tell you – she saw them and told me all about it in her letters. My son Philip was here with her when the last one arrived. Something drove the whales right across the Equator into these seas. Something drove them to cast themselves up on to this beach, raking their stomachs open on the reefs as they did so, to die where you see them lying now. Hang around ten days, Theo, till the next full moon. You may see another cetaceous suicide.'

There were crabs working in the sand among the barred shadows of the rib cage, burrowing and signalling to each other. When Devlin spoke, anger was back in his voice.

'Okay, you clever trawlerman, tell me the answer to the riddle. It's been revealed to you alone, I suppose, why they killed themselves?'

'They were suffering from side effects, Theo. The side effects of the immortality disease. You know the Baltic virus seems to bring long life – but you haven't had time to find out what else it brings. You've been in so much of a hurry you abandoned scientific method. You didn't want to get any older before you infected yourself. You didn't allow a proper trial period. You may be going to live a thousand years – *but what else is going to happen to you?* What happened to these poor creatures so awful that they could not bear their increase of years? Whatever it was, it was terrible, and soon it will be overtaking you, and all your conspirators sweating it out uneasily in Naples!'

The silencer was extremely effective. The pistol made only a slight hiss, rather like a man blowing a strawberry pip from between his teeth. The bullet made a louder noise as it ricochetted off a bleached rib and sped over the ocean. Suddenly Yale was full of movement, moving faster than he had moved in years, lunging forward. He hit Devlin before he fired again. They fell into the sand. Yale on top. He got his foot over Devlin's arm, grasped him by both hands by the windpipe, and bashed his head repeatedly in the sand. When the gun slid loose, he stopped what he was doing, picked up the weapon, and climbed to his feet. Puffing a little, he brushed the sand from his old jeans.

'It wasn't graceful,' he said, glaring down at the purple-faced man rolling at his feet. 'You're a fool!' With a last indignant slap at his legs, he turned and headed back for the coral-built house.

Caterina ran out in terror at the sight of him. The natives surged towards him, thought better of it, and cleared a way for him to pass.

'Clem, Clem, what have you done? You've not shot him?'

'I want a glass of lemonade. It's all right, Cat, my love .. He isn't really hurt.'

When he was sitting down at the table in the cool and drinking the lemonade she mixed him, he began to shake. She had the sense not to say anything until he was ready to speak. She stood beside him, stroking his neck. Presently they saw through the window Devlin coming staggering over the dunes. Without looking in their direction, he made his way over to the helicopter. With Thomas's aid, he climbed in, and in a few moments the engine started and the blades began to turn. The machine lifted, and they watched in silence as it whirled away over the water, eastwards towards the Indian sub-continent. The sound of it died and soon the sight of it was swallowed up in the gigantic sky.

'He was another whale. He came to wreck himself here.'

'You'll have to send a signal to London and tell them everything, won't you?'

'You're right. And tomorrow I must catch some jewfish. I suspect they may be picking up the infection.'

He looked askance at his wife. She had put on her dark glasses, while he was gone. Now she took them off again and sat by him, regarding him anxiously.

'I'm not a saint, Cat. Never suggest that again. I'm a bloody liar. I had to tell Theo an awful lie about why the whales ran themselves up our beach.'

'Why?'

'I don't know! Whales have been beaching themselves for years and nobody knows why. Theo would have remembered that if he hadn't been so scared.'

'I mean, why lie to him? You should only lie to people you respect, my mother used to say.'

He laughed. 'Good for her! I lied to scare him. Everyone is going to know about the immortality virus in a few weeks, and I suspect they're all going to want to be infected. I want them all scared. Then perhaps they'll pause and think what they're asking for – the length of many lifetimes living with their first lifetime's inadequacies.'

31

'Theo's taking your lie with him. You want that to circulate with the virus?'

He started to clean his spectacles on his handkerchief.

'I do.' The world is about to undergo a drastic and radical change. The more slowly that change takes place, the more chance we – all living things, I mean, as well as you and I – have of living quiet and happy as well as lengthy lives. My lie may act as a sort of brake on change. People ought to think what a terrifying thing immortality is – it means sacrificing the mysteries of death. Now how about a bathe, just as if nothing revolutionary had happened?'

As they changed into their swim things, as she stood divested of her clothes, Caterina said, 'I've suddenly had a vision, Clem. Please, I've changed my mind – I want to, I want us both to live as long as we possibly can. I'll sacrifice death for life. You know what I did with Philip? It was only because I suddenly felt my youth slipping from me. Time was against me. I got desperate. With more time . . . well, all our values would change, wouldn't they?'

He nodded and said simply, 'You're right, of course.'

They both began to laugh, out of pleasure and excitement. Laughing, they ran down to the lapping ocean, and for a moment it was as if Yale had left all his hesitations behind with his clothes.

As they sat on the edge of the water and snapped their flippers on, he said, 'Sometimes I understand things about people. Theo came here to silence me. But he is an effective man and he was so ineffectual today. It must mean that at bottom he really came to see you, just as you guessed at the time – I reckon he wanted company in all that limitless future he opened up for himself.'

As they sliced out side by side into the warm water, she said without surprise, 'We need time together, Clem, to understand each other.'

They dived together, down in a trail of bubbles below the sparkling surface, startling the fish. Flipping over on his side, Yale made for the channel that led out to the open sea. She followed, glad in her heart, as she was destined to do and be for the next score and half of centuries.

...AND THE
STAGNATION OF THE
HEART

Under the weight of sunlight, the low hills abased themselves. To the three people sitting behind the driver of the hover, it seemed that pools of liquid – something between oil and water – formed constantly on the pitted road ahead, to disappear miraculously as they reached the spot. In all the landscape, this optical illusion was the only hint that moisture existed.

The passengers had not spoken for some while. Now the Pakistani Health Official, Firoz Ayub Khan, turned to his guests and said, 'Within an hour, we shall be into Calcutta. Let us hope and pray that the air-conditioning of this miserable machine holds out so long!'

The woman by his side gave no sign that she heard him, continuing to stare forward through her dark glasses; she left it to her husband to make an appropriate response. She was a slender woman of dark complexion, her narrow face made notable by its generous mouth. Her black hair, gathered over one shoulder, was disordered from the four-hour drive down from the hill station.

Her husband was a tall spare man, apparently in his midforties, who wore old-fashioned steel-rimmed spectacles. His face in repose carried an eroded look, as if he had spent many years gazing at just such countries as the one outside. He said, 'It was good of you to consent to letting us use this slow mode of transport, Dr Khan. I appreciate your impatience to get back to work.'

'Well, well, I am impatient, that is perfectly true. Calcutta

33

needs me – and you, too, now you are recovered from your illness. And Mrs Yale also, naturally.' It was difficult to determine whether's Khan's voice concealed sarcasm.

'It is well worth seeing the land at first hand, in order to appreciate the magnitude of the problems against which Pakistan and India are battling.'

Clement Yale had noted before that his speeches intended to mollify the health official seemed to produce the opposite effect. Khan said: 'Mr Yale, what problems do you refer to? There is no problem anywhere, only the old satanic problem of the human condition, that is all.'

'I was referring to the evacuation of Calcutta and its attendant difficulties. You would admit they constituted a problem, surely?'

This sort of verbal jostling had broken out during the last half-hour of the ride.

'Well, well, naturally where you have a city containing some twenty-five million people, there you expect to find a few problems, wouldn't you agree, Mrs Yale? Rather satanic problems, maybe – but always stemming from and rooted in the human condition. That is why executives such as ourselves are always needed, isn't it?'

Yale gestured beyond the window, where broken carts lay by the roadside. 'This is the first occasion in modern times that a city has simply bogged itself down and had to be abandoned. I would call that a special problem.'

He hardly listened to Khan's long and complicated answer; the health official was always involving himself in contradictions from which verbiage could not rescue him. He stared instead out of the window as the irreparable world of heat slid past. The carts and cars had been fringing the road for some while – indeed, almost all the way from the hospital in the hills, where East Madras was still green. Here, nearer Calcutta, their skeletal remains lay thicker. Between the shafts of some of the carts lay bones, many of them no longer recognizable as those of bullocks; lesser skeletons toothed the wilderness beyond the road.

The hover-driver muttered constantly to himself. The dead formed no obstacle to their progress; the living and half-living had yet to be considered. Pouring out of the great antheap ahead were knots of human beings, solitary figures, family groups, men, women, children, the more fortunate with beasts of burden or handcarts or bicycles to support themselves or their scanty belongings. Blindly they moved forward, going

34

they hardly knew whither, treading over those who had fallen, not raising their heads to avoid the oncoming hover-ambulance.

For centuries, the likes of these people had been pouring into Calcutta from the dying hinterland. Nine months ago, when the government of the city had fallen and the Indian Congress had announced that the city would be abandoned, the stream had reversed its direction. The refugees became refugees again.

Caterina behind her dark glasses took in the parched images. Mankind driven always driven the bare foot on the way the eternal road of earth and no real destination only the way to water and longer grass. Will we be able to get a drink there always the stone beneath the passing instep.

She said, 'I suppose one shouldn't hope for a shower when we get there.'

Ayub Khan said: 'The air-conditioning is not all it should be, lady. Hence the sensation of heat. There has not been proper servicing of the vehicle. I shall make some appropriate complaints when we arrive, never wonder!'

Jerking to avoid a knot of refugees, the hover rounded a shoulder of the hill. The endless deltaic plain of the Ganges stretched before them, fading in the far distance, annihilating itself in its own vision of sun.

To one side of the track stood a grim building, the colour of mud, its walls rising silent and stark. Not a fortress, not a temple: the meaningless functionalism, now functionless, of some kind of factory. Beside it, one or two goats scampered and vanished.

Ayub Khan uttered a command to the driver. The hover slid to one side. The road near at hand was temporarily deserted. Their machine bumped over the ditch and drifted towards the factory, raising dust high as it went. Its engines died, it sank to the ground. Ayub Khan was reaching behind him for the holstered rifle on the rack above their heads.

'What's this place?' Yale asked, rousing himself.

'A temporary diversion, Mr Yale, that will not occupy us for more than the very moment. Maybe you and your lady will care to climb out with me for a moment and exercise? Go steadily, remembering you were ill.'

'I have no wish to climb out, Dr Khan. We are urgently needed in Calcutta. What are we stopping for? What is this place?'

The Pakistani doctor smiled and took down a box of cartridges. As he loaded the rifle, he said: 'I forget you are not only recently

35

sick but are also immortal and must take the greatest care. But the desperate straits of Calcutta will wait for us for ten minutes break, I assure you. Recall, the human condition goes on for ever.'

The human condition goes on for ever sticks stones bows and arrows shotguns nuclear weapons quescharges and the foot and face going down into the dust the perfect place for death. She stirred and said, 'The human condition goes on for ever, Dr Khan, but we are expected in Dalhousie Square today.'

As he opened the door, he smiled. 'Expectancy is a pleasing part of our life, Mrs Yale.'

The Yales looked at each other. The driver was climbing down after Ayub Khan, and gesticulating excitedly. 'His relish of power likewise,' Yale said.

'We cadged the ride.'

'The ride – not the moralizing! Still, part of abrasion.'

'Feeling right, Clem?'

'Perfectly.' To show her, he climbed out of the vehicle with a display of energy. He was still angry with himself for contracting cholera in the middle of a job where every man's capacity was stretched to the utmost: the dying metropolis was a stewpot of disease.

As he helped Cat down, they felt the heat of the plains upon them. It was the heat of a box, allowing no perspectives but its own. The moisture in it stifled their lungs; with each breath, they felt their shoulders prickle and their bodies weep.

Ayub Khan was striding forward, rifle ready for action, the driver chattering excitedly by him, carrying spare ammunition.

Time, suffering from a slow wound, was little past midday, so that the derelict factory was barren of shadow. Nevertheless, the two English moved instinctively towards it, following the Pakistanis, feeling as they went old heat rebuffed from the walls of the great fossil.

'Old cement factory.'

'Cementary.'

'Mortarl remaniés . . .'

'Yes, here's an acre stone indeed . . .'

The rifle went off loudly.

'Missed!' said Ayub Khan cheerfully, rubbing the top of his head with his free hand. He ran forward, the driver close behind him. Ramshackle remains of a metal outbuilding stood to one side of the factory façade; a powdered beam of it collapsed as the men trotted past and disappeared from view.

And the termites too have their own empires and occasions and never over-extend their capacities they create and destroy on a major time-scale yet they have no aspirations. Man became sick when he discovered he lived on a planet when his world became finite his aspirations grew infinite and what the hell could those idiots be doing?

Switching on his pocket fan, Yale walked up the gritty steps of the factory. The double wooden door, once barred, had long since been broken down. He paused on the threshold and looked back at his wife, standing indecisively in the heat.

'Coming in?'

She made an impatient gesture and followed. He watched her. He had watched that walk for almost four centuries now, still without tiring of it. It was *her* walk: independent, yet not entirely: self-conscious, yet, in a true sense, self-forgetting; a stride that did not hurry, that was neither old nor young; a woman's walk; Cat's walk; a cat-walk. It defined her as clearly as her voice. He realized that in the preoccupations of the last two months, in doomed Calcutta and in the hospital ward, he had often forgotten her, the living her.

As she came up the steps level with him, he took her arm.

'Feelings?'

'Specifiably, irritation with Khan foremost. Secondarily, knowledge we need our Khans . . .'

'Yes, but how now to you?'

'Our centuries – as ever. Limit gravely areas of non-predictability in human relations among Caucasian-Christian community. Consequent accumulation of staleness *abraded* by unknown factors.'

'Such as Khan?'

'Sure. You similarly abraded, Clem?'

'He has chafage value. Ditto all sub-continent.'

His fingers released her arm. The brown flesh ever young left no sign of the ephemeral touch. But the Baltic virus would have quickly healed the harshest grip he could have bestowed.

They looked into the old chaos of the factory, moved in over rubble. A corpse lay in a side office, open-mouthed, hollow, without stink; something slid away from under, afraid for its own death.

From the passage beyond, noise, echoey and conflicting.

'Back to the float?'

'This old temple to India's failure – ' He stopped. Two small goats, black of face and beardless, came at a smart clip from the back of the darkness ahead, eyes – in Ayub Khan's pet word – 'satanic', came forward swerving and bleating.

And from the far confusion of shadow, Ayub Khan stepped and raised his rifle. Yale lifted a hand as the shot came.

Temples and the conflicting desires to make and destroy ascetic priests and fat ones, my loving husband still had his tender core unspoilt for more years.

The goats tumbling past them, Yale sagging to the ground, the noise of the shot with enormous power to extend itself far into the future. Cat transfixed, and somewhere a new ray of light searching down as if part of the roof had given way.

Rushing forward, Ayub Khan gave Cat back her ability to move; she turned to Yale, who was already getting to his feet again. The Pakistani calling, his driver behind him.

'My dear and foolish Mr Yale! Have I not rifled you, I sincerely trust! What terrible disaster if you are dead! How did I know you crept secretly into this place? My godfathers! How you did scare me! Driver! *Pani lao, jhaldi!*'

He fussed anxiously about Yale until the driver returned from the ambulance with a beaker of water. Yale drank it and said: 'Thank you, I'm perfectly well, Dr Khan, and you missed me, fortunately.'

'What do you imagine you were doing?' Cat asked.

Hold your hands together so they will not shake and your thighs if he had been killed murder most dreaded of crimes even to short-livers and this idiot –

'Madam, you must surely see that I was shooting at the two goats. Though I hope thoroughly that I am a good Muslim, I was shooting at those two damned satanic goats. That action needs not any justification, surely?'

She was still shaking and trying to recover her poise. High abrasion value okay! 'Goats? In here?'

'Mrs Yale, the driver and I have seen these goats from the road and chase after them. Because the back of this factory is broken, they escape from us into here. We follow. Little do we know that you creep secretly in from the front! What a scare! My godfathers!'

As he paused to light a mescahale, she saw his hand was shaking; the observation restored a measure of sympathy for the man. She further relaxed her pulse-count by a side-glance at Yale, for their glances by now, cryptic as their personal conversations, told them as much; certain the shot was careless, he was already more interested in the comedy of Ayub Khan's reactions than his own.

Yes, many would find him a negative man not seeing that the truth is he has the ability to add to his own depths other people's. He stands there while others talk saintly later he will deliver the nub of the matter. My faith of which he would disapprove indeed I have an obligation not to be all faith must also fill my abrasion quota for him!

'You know, I really hate these little satanic goats! In Pakistan and India they cause the chief damage to territory and the land will never revive while goats are upon it. In my own province, I watch them climb the trees to eat up new tender shoots. So the latest laws to execute goats, reinforced with rewards of two new-rupees per hoof, are so much to my thinking, more than you Europeans can understand . . .'

'That is certainly true, Dr Khan,' Yale said. 'I fully share your dislike of the destructive power of the goat. Unfortunately, such animals are a part and parcel of our somewhat patchy history. The hogs that ensured that the early forests, once felled by stone axes, did not grow again, and the sheep and goats that formed man's traditional food supplies, have left as indelible a mark on Europe as on Asia and elsewhere. The eroded shores of the Mediterranean and the barren lands all round that sea are their doing, in league with man.'

Does the pressure of my thought make him speak of early mankind now? Through these centuries glad and stern I have come to see man's progress as a blind attempt to escape from those hopeful buffoons so exposed to chance yet chance beats down like weather whatever you cover your back with we know who live a long while that the heart stagnates without abrasion and the great abrader is chance.

Now Ayub Khan had perked up and was smiling over the fumes of his mescahale, gesturing with one hand.

'Now, now, don't be bitter, Mr Yale – nobody denies that the Europeans have their share of minor troubles! But let's admit while we are being really frank that they also have all the luck, don't they? I mean to say, to give one example, the Baltic virus happened in their part of the world, didn't it? just like the Industrial Revolution many hundreds of years ago.'

39

'Your part of the world, Doctor, has enough to contend with without longevity as well!'

'Precisely so! What is an advantage to you Europeans, and to the Americans behind their long disgraceful isolationism, is a disadvantage entirely to the unlucky Asiatic nations, that is what I am saying. That is precisely why our governments have made longevity illegal – as you well know, a Pakistani suffers capital punishment if he is found to be a long-liver, just because we do not solve our satanic population problem so very easily as Europe. So we are condemned to our life-expectancy of merely forty-seven years average, against your thousands! How can that be fair, Mr Yale? We are all human beings, wherever we live on the planet of Earth, equator or pole, my godfathers!'

Yale shrugged. 'I don't pretend to call it fair. Nobody calls it fair. It just happens that "fairness" is not a built-in natural law. Man invented the concept of justice – it's one of his better ideas – but the rest of the universe, unfortunately, doesn't give a damn for it.'

'It's very easy for you to be smug.'

He looks so angry and hurt his skin almost purple his eyeballs yellow rather like a goat himself not a good representative of his race. But the antipathy can never be overcome the haves and the have-nots the Neanderthal and the Cro-Magnon the rich and the poor we can never give what we have. We should get back into the float and drive on. I'd like to wash my hair. The goats moved endlessly across the plain with every step they took the great enchanted ruin behind them crumbled into a material like straw and as they went and multiplied long grasses sprang out of the human corpses littering the plain and the goats capered forward and ate.

'Smugness does not enter the matter. There are the facts and – '

'Facts! Facts! Oh, your satanic British factualism! I suppose you call the many goats facts? How does it come about, ask yourself, how does it come about that these goats can live forever and I cannot, for all my superior reasoning powers?'

Yale said, 'I fear I can only answer you with more factualism. We know now, as for many years we did not, that the Baltic virus is extraterrestrial in origin, most probably arriving on this planet by tektite. To exist in a living organism, the virus needs a certain rare dynamic condition in the mito-chondria of cells known as rubmission – the Red Vibrations of the popular press

40

– and this it finds in only a handful of terrestrial types, among which are such disparate creatures as copepods, Adelie penguins, herring, man, and goats and sheep.'

'We have enough trouble with this satanic drought without immortal goats!'

'Immortality – as you call longevity – is not proof against famine. Although the goats' reproductive period is in theory infinitely extended, they are still dying for lack of nourishment.'

'Not so fast as the humans!'

'Vigilance will certainly be needed when the rains come.'

'You immortals can afford to wait that long!'

'We are *long-livers*, Dr Khan.'

'My godfathers, define for me the difference between longevity and immortality in a way that makes sense to a short-lived Pakistan man!'

'Immortality can afford to forget death and, in consequence, the obligations of life. Longevity can't.'

'Let's get on to Calcutta,' Cat said. Vultures perched on the top of the stained façade: she found herself vulnerable to their presence. She walked across to the doorway. The driver had already slipped out at the back of the factory.

On the long road the humble figures. When did that woman last have a bath to have to bear children in such conditions. This is what life is all about this is why we left the stainless towers of our cooler countries their comforts and compromises in the brokendown parts of the world there is no pretence about what life is really like Clem and I and the other long-livers are merely clever western artefacts of suspended decay everyday we know that one day we shall have to tumble into slag each our own Calcutta oh for god's sake satanically can it!

The men were following her. She saw now that Ayub Khan had laid a hand on Yale's arm and was talking in more friendly fashion.

The hover's door had been left open. It would be abominably hot in there.

Two skeletal goats crossed the road, ears lop, parading before two refugees. The refugees were men walking barefoot with sticks, bags of belongings slung on their backs. For them, the goats would represent not only food but the reward the government offered for hooves. Breaking from their trance, they waved their arms and wielded their sticks. One of the goats was struck across its serrated backbone. It broke into a trot. Ayub Khan raised his rifle and fired at the other goat from almost point-blank range.

He hit it in the stomach. The creature's back legs collapsed. Piddling blood, it attempted to drag itself off the road, away from Ayub Khan. The two refugees fell on it, jostling each other with scarecrow gestures. With an angry shout, Ayub Khan ran forward and prodded them out of the way with the rifle barrel. He called to the driver, who came at a trot, pulling out a knife; squatting, he chopped at the goat's legs repeatedly until the hooves were severed; by that time, the animal appeared to be dead.

The government will pay. Like all Indian legislation this bounty favours the rich and the strong at the expense of the poor and weak. Like everything else cool Delhi justice melts in the heat.

Above the factory entrance, the vultures shuffled and nodded in understanding.

Straightening, Ayub Khan gestured to the two refugees, inviting them to drag the body off. They stood stupidly, not coming forward, perhaps fearing attack. Clapping his hands once, Ayub Kahn dismissed them and turned away, circling the goat's carcass.

To Caterina he said, 'Just allow me one further moment, madam, while I shoot down this second goat. It is my public duty.'

To sit in the shade of the ambulance or go and watch him carry out his public duty. No choice really he shall not think us squeamish we don't need his uncouth exhibition to tell us that even we are in the general league with death. Remember after Clem and I returned from the bullfight in Seville Philip no more than seven years old I suppose asked Who won? and cried when we laughed. We must be brave bulls *toros bravos* who live on something less prone to eclipse than hope.

Yale said, 'Follow and these can at least claim what's left.'

'Sure, and we attend caprine execution.'

'Gory caprice!'

'Goat kaputt.'

'You over-hot?'

'Just delay. Thanks.' Smiles in the general blindness.

'Delay product of no goal within fulfilment.'

'Vice versa, too, suppose.'

'Suppose. Eastern thing. Hence Industrial Rev never took here.'

'Factory example, Clem.'

'So, quite. Wrongly situated regards supply, power, consumers, distribution.'

Calcutta itself a similar example on enormous satanic scale. Situated on Hooghli, river now almost entirely silted up despite dramatic attempts. And the centuries-old division between India and Pakistan like a severed limb the refugees breaking down all attempts at organization finally the water-table under the city hopelessly poisoned by sewage mass eruptions of disease scampering mesolithic men crouched in their cave exchanging illnesses viruses use mankind as walking cities.

'Calcutta somewhat ditto.'

'Ssh, founded by East India merchant, annoy Khan!'

They looked at each other, just perceptibly grinning, as they walked round to the back of the factory.

The surviving goat was white-bodied, marked with brown specks; its head and face were dark brown or black, its eyes yellow. It walked under a series of low *bashas*, now deserted, apparently once used as huts for the factory-workers. Their thatched walls, ruinous, gave them an air of transparency. The light speared them. Beyond them, the undistinguished lump of Calcutta lay amid the nebulous areas where land met sky.

Ravenously, the goat reached up and dragged at the palm leaves covering a *basha* roof. As a section of the roof came down in a cascade of dust, Ayub Khan fired. Kicking up its bounty-laden heels, the goat disappeared among the huts.

Ayub Khan reloaded. 'Generally, I am a satanically sound marksman. It is this confounded heat putting me off that I chiefly complain of. Why don't you have a shot, Yale, and see if you do a lot better? You English are such sportsmen!' He offered the rifle.

'No, thanks, Doctor. I'm rather anxious for us to be getting on to Calcutta.'

'Calcutta is just a tragedy – let it wait, let it wait! The hunting blood is up! First, let's have a little fun with this terrible satanic goat!'

'Fun? It was public duty a moment ago!'

Ayub Khan looked at him. 'What are you doing here, anyway, with your pretty wife? Isn't this all *fun* for you as well as a public duty? Did you have to come to our satanic Asia, ask yourself?'

43

Isn't he right don't we eternally have to redeem ourselves for the privilege of living and seeing other life by sacrificing death Clement must have said the same thing often to himself by sacrificing death did we not also sacrifice the norms of normal life in this long-protracted life is not our atonement our fun helping supervise the evacuation of Calcutta our goat-shoot. In his eyes we can never redeem ourselves only in our own eyes.

'Instead of papering over the cracks at home, Doctor, we prefer to stand on the brink of your chasms. You must forgive us. Go and shoot your goat and then we will proceed to Calcutta.'

'It is very curious that when you seem to be talking better sense, I am not able to understand you. Driver, *idhar ao*!'

Gesturing to the driver, the health official disappeared behind the threadbare huts.

On the road, the refugees still trod, losing themselves in the mists of distance and time. Individuality was forgotten: there were only organisms, moving according to certain laws, performing antique motions. In the Hooghli, water flowed, bringing down silt from source to delta, the dredgers rusting, the arteries clogging, little speckled crabs waving across grey sandbanks.

Poul Anderson

HIGH TREASON

In three hours by the clock they will be here to kill me. The door will crack open. Two noncoms will step through and flank it, in parade uniforms with stunners at the ready. I don't know whether their faces will wear loathing and righteousness, or that sick pity I have observed on some aboard this ship, but it is certain that they will be pathetically young, because all the enlisted ratings are. Then Erik Halvorsen will stride in between them and come to attention. So will I. 'Edward Breckinridge,' he will say like a machine, and proceed with the formula. Not so long ago he called me Ed, and we were messmates, and on our last leave we went on a drinking bout which must by now have become a part of the local mythology. (This was in Port Desire, but next day we flitted down to the sea, which is golden coloured on that planet, and tumbled in the surf and lay on the sand letting sunlight and thunder possess us.) I don't know what will be in his eyes either. Curious, that one's closest male friend should be so unpredictable. But since he was always a good officer, he can be counted on to play his role out.

So can I. There is no gain in breaking the ritual, and ample reason for not doing so. Perhaps I should not even have dismissed the chaplain. With so much religiosity about, as our universe goes down in wreck, I have painted myself more strongly Lucifer by not spending these last hours in prayer. Will my children hear at school. He wasn't just a traitor, he was a dirty atheist – ? Never mind. I am not entitled to a great deal, but let me claim the dignity of remaining myself.

There will also be a kind of dignity in what follows: barbaric, macabre, and necessary. I will march down the corridor between the stiff bodies and stiffer faces of men I commanded; drums will drown the mutter of engines and priest. The inner airlock door will already stand wide. I will enter the chamber. The door will close. Then, for a moment, I can be alone. I shall try to hold to me the memory of Alice and the children, but perhaps my sweat will stink too harshly.

They don't pump the air out of the chamber in cases like this. That would be cruel. They simply pull the emergency switch. (No, not 'they'. One man's hand must do it. But whose? I don't want to know.) An engine will strain against the atmospheric pressure, one kilogram per square centimetre that we have borne with us, along with salt blood and funny little patches of hair and funny little instincts, all the way from Earth. The outer door will swing. Suddenly my coffin brims with darkness and stars. Earth's air rejects me. I fly out. The ship resumes hyper-drive.

For me, then, the universe will no longer ever have been.

But I ramble. It was well meant of them to give me this psychograph. The written word lies, the distorted molecules of a thought-recording tape do not. My apologia can be analysed for sincerity as well as logic. The worlds will be assured that I was at least an honest fool, which could make things easier for Alice, Jeanne, small Bobby who – her last letter said – has begun to look like his father. On the other hand, being no expert in the use of the machine, I will commit more of myself to the record than I like.

Well, keep trying, Ed, old chap. You can always wipe the tape. Though why you should be concerned about your privacy, when you are going to be dead –

Drusilla.

NO.

Go away. Take back your summer-scented hair, the feel of breasts and belly, the bird that sang in the garden beyond your window, take them back, Alice is my girl, and I'd simply been away from her too long, and no, that isn't true either, I damn well had fun with you, Dru, my puss, and I don't regret a microsecond of our nights but it would hurt Alice to know, or would she understand, Christ-Osiris-Baldr-Xipe, I can't even be sure about that.

Get your mind back to higher things. Like battle. Quite okay to kill, you know, it's love which is dangerous and must be kept on tight leash, no, now I'm knee-jerking like one of those Brotherhood types. The soldier is akin to the civil monitor, both trained in violence because violence is sometimes necessary for the purposes of society. My problem was, what do you do when those purposes become impossible of attainment?

You fight. The Morwain will not forget either, certain hours amidst the blaze of Cantrell's Cluster. Part of my defence, remember, Erik Halvorsen? – my squadron inflicted heavy damage on the enemy – but the court martial couldn't follow such logic. Why did I attack a superior force after betraying a planet . . . a species? My claim is on record, that in my considered judgement the mission on which we had been ordered would have had catastrophic results, but that something might have been accomplished by striking elsewhere. Be it said, though, here to the ultimate honesty of this machine, I hoped to be captured. I have no more death wish than you, Erik.

And *someone* will have to represent men, when the Morwain come. Why not myself?

One reason why not, among others: Hideki Iwasaki. (I mean Iwasaki Hideki, the Japanese put the surname first, we're such a richly variant life form.) 'Yahhh!' he screamed when we took our direct hit. I saw the control turret flare with lightnings, I saw him penetrated, through earthquake shudder in the ship and a whistle of departing air that pierced my helmet, my phones heard him scream.

Then darkness clapped down upon us. The gee-field had gone dead too, I floated, whirling until I caromed off a bulkhead and caught a stanchion. My mouth was full of blood, which tasted like wet iron. As the dazzle cleared from my retinae, I saw the master panel shine blue, emergency lighting, and Hideki outlined before it. I knew him by the number fluorescing on his armour. Air gushed from him, as fast as the tank could replace it white with condensing moisture, mingled with blood in thick separate globules. I thought amidst my pulses, gloriously, why, we're disabled. Totally. We haven't gone on to standby control, we're rudderless in space, the switchover circuits must be fused. We can only surrender. Plug in your jack quick, man, raise Comcenter and order the capitulation signal broadcast. No, wait. First you pass command on formally, to Feinstein aboard the *Yorktown*, so that the squadron may proceed with its battle. But then you're out of action. You'll come home with the Morwain.

47

Iwasaki's gauntlets moved. He had tools in them. Dying, he floated in front of the smitten superconductor brain and made a jackleg repair. It didn't take long. Just a matter of a few connections, so that the standby system could get the order to take over. I should have thought of trying it myself. That I did not, well, yes, I admit that that was my real treason. But when I saw what he was doing, I shoved myself to him, along with Mboto and Ghopal, and lent a hand.

We couldn't do much. He was the electronics officer. Besides, as for me, his blood drifted across my faceplate and fogged it. But we passed him what he needed from the tool kit. By the blue light, through the black smears, I saw his face a little drained of everything but sweat and will. He did not permit himself to die until he had finished.

The lights came back on. So did weight. And the viewscreens. And the audio inductors. We'd have to get along on tanked air until we could shift to the other turret. I looked into space. The stars were thick here, heartlessly brilliant against black, but sharpest was a flash half a million kilometres away. And: '¡*Por Dios!*' cried the evaluation officer, 'she was a Jango cruiser! Someone's put a missile in her!'

Turned out the *Agincourt* had done so. I hear her captain has been cited for a medal. Is he grateful to me?

At the moment, though, I knew only that Iwasaki had resurrected the *Syrtis Minor* and I must therefore continue to fight her. I called for the medics to come see if they could resurrect him too. He was a good little man, who had shyly shown me pictures of his good little children, under the cherry trees of Kyoto. But later I heard there was no chance for him. With normal hospital facilities, he could have been hooked into a machine until a new gastro-intestinal tract had been grown; however, warships haven't room or mass to spare for such gadgets.

I plugged myself back into control. Reports snapped through my ears, numbers flickered before my eyes, I made my decisions and issued my orders. But chiefly I was conscious of a background whine in my phones, blood and a little vomit on my tongue. We were not going to be captured after all.

Instead, we fought free and returned to base, what was left of us.

I wonder if military men have always been intellectuals. It

isn't in their legend. Rather, we think of headlong Alexander, methodical Caesar, Napoleon stumping across Europe, Malanowicz and his computers. But shouldn't we likewise remember Aristotle, the Julian calender, the Code, the philosophical project? At any rate, when you fight across interstellar distances, for commonwealths embodying whole planetary systems, you have to understand the machines which make it possible; you have to try to understand races as sentient as man, but separated from us by three or four thousand million years of evolution; you even have to know something about man himself, lest minds fall to pieces out yonder. So the average officer today is better educated and has done a good bit more thinking than the average Brother of Love.

Oh, that Brotherhood! I wish they could have sat, dirt and self-righteousness and the whole dismal works, in Colonel Goncharov's class.

Sunlight slanted across Academy lawns, lost itself among oak leaves, emerged to glance off a cannon which had fired at Trafalgar, and struck the comets upon his shoulders. I sat and worshipped, at first, for he had won the Lunar Crescent before I was born. But then he asked me to do what was harder.

'Gentlemen,' he said, in that slow, accented Esperanto which was such a joke in our barracks – and he leaned across his desk, balanced on fingertips, and the sun touched his hair also, it was still rust colour, and made shadows in the creases of his face; and, yes, a smell of green (E)arth blew in, with the sleepy noise of a mower somewhere in the middle distance – 'gentlemen, you have heard a good many fine words about honour, esprit de corps, and service to mankind. They are true enough. But you will not live up to them unless you can see your service in its proper perspective. The Cosmocorps is not the élite of human society, its mission is not the purpose of society, it must not expect the highest material rewards or even the highest honours which society has to offer.

'We are an instrument.

'Man is not alone in this universe. Nor is he entitled to every habitable world. There are other races, with their own hopes and ambitions, their own pains and fears; they look out of other eyes and they think other thoughts, but their aims are no less legitimate to them than ours are to us. It is well when we can be friends with them.

'But that isn't forever possible. Some of you will explain it by original sin, some by Karma, some by simple mortal fallibility. The fact remains that societies do conflict. In such cases, one must try to negotiate the dispute. And true negotiation can only take place between equals. Therefore equality in the capability of inflicting harm, as well as in other and higher capabilities, is essential. I do not say this is good, I say merely that it is so. You are to become part of the instrument which gives Earth and the Union that capability.

'An instrument can be misused. A hammer can drive a nail or crush a skull. All too often, armies have been similarly misused. But the fact that you have accepted military discipline and will presently accept commissions does not absolve you from your responsibilities as citizens.

'*Read* your Clausewitz. War is not an end but a continuation of political intercourse. The most horrible disasters of a horrible history occurred when that was forgotten. Your duty as officers – a duty too high and difficult to be included in the Articles – will be to remember.'

I suppose that basically I am a humourless type. I like a joke as well as you do, I rather distinguish myself in my class by my fund of limericks, a poker game or a drinking bout is fun, but I do take some things with a possibly priggish seriousness.

Like this matter of racial hatred. I will no more tolerate that word 'Jango' than I would have tolerated 'Nigger' or 'Gook' a few centuries ago. (You see, I've read quite a lot of history. Hobby of mine, and a way to pass the long time between stars.) It was brought against me at the court martial. Tom Deare testified that I had spoken well of the Morwain. They were fair minded men on the board, who reprimanded him and struck his words from the record, but – Tom, you were my friend. Weren't you?

Let me set straight what happened. Memory gets more total with every sweep of that minute hand. We were on Asphodel for refitting. Once this was the pet hope of every spaceman. Next to Earth herself, perhaps more so for many, Asphodel! (Yes, yes, I know it's an entire world, with ice caps and deserts and stinking swamps, but I mean the part we humans made our own, in those magnificent days when we thought we had the freedom of the galaxy, and could pick and choose our colony sites.) Mountains shouldering white into a cornflower sky, valleys one dazzle of blossoms and bird wings, the little laughterful towns and the

50

girls . . . But this was late in the war. You hated to go out after dark, for the enemy held those stars. Most of the towns were already empty, doors creaked in the wind, echoes rang hollow from your footfall in the streets. Now and then a thunder-clap rolled, another ferry taking off with another load of civilians for evacuation. Asphodel fell to the Morwain two months afterward.

We sat in a deserted tavern, Tom and I, violating regs by drinking liquor which could not be taken away. There was nothing else to do. War is mostly hurry up and wait. Sunlight came in, and the same green smell I remembered across an eon, and a dog ran by outside, abandoned, bewildered, hungry.

'Oh, God *damn* them!' Tom shouted into silence.

'Who?' I asked, pouring myself a refill. 'If you mean those officious bastards in Q M, I entirely agree, but aren't you wishing a rather large job on to the Almighty?'

'This is no time to be funny,' he said.

'It's no time to be anything else,' I answered. We had just heard about the destruction of the Ninth Fleet.

'The Jangos,' he said. 'The filthy, slimy, slithering, pervert-begotten Jangos.'

'The Morwain, you mean,' I said. I was rather drunk too, or I would simply have held my peace. But it buzzed in my brain. 'They aren't filthy. Cleaner by instinct than we are. You don't see litter in their cities. Their perspiration is glutinous, they walk like cats, and they have three sexes, but what of it?'

'What *of* it?' He raised a fist. His features had gone white, except for two fever-spots on the cheekbones. 'They're going to take over the universe and you ask what of it?'

'Who says they're going to?'

'The news, you clotbrain!'

I couldn't answer directly, so I said, with that exaggerated consciousness of each single word which comes at a certain stage of drink: 'Earth-type planets are none too common, they wanted the same real estate we did. Border disputes led to war. Now their announced purpose is to draw Earth's teeth, just as ours was to draw theirs. But they haven't said anything about throwing us off the planets – most of the planets – we already hold. That'd be too costly.'

'No, it wouldn't. They'll only need to massacre our colonials.'

'Would we massacre – what's the figure? – about twenty

thousand million in either case – would we massacre that many thinking creatures?'

'I'd like to,' he got out between his teeth.

'Look,' I said, 'forget the propaganda. As the war dragged on, and went badly, we've lost all sense of proportion. Suppose they do occupy us?'

'Those tentacled horrors,' he whispered, 'under the spires of Oxford.'

Well, for me it would be strangers walking the Wyoming earth where free men once whooped their cattle down the long trail; and for Iwasaki, demon shapes gaping before Buddha at Kamajura; and for Goncharov, if he was unfortunate enough to be still alive, an alien victory monument raised in the holy Kremlin; and on and on, mans-history's tapestry warped into a shape our dead would never have recognized. But – 'They'll set up a government, if they win,' I told him, 'and we'll have to learn some new ways of thinking. But you know, I've studied them, and I met some of them before the war and got pretty friendly, and you know, they admire a lot about us.'

He sat altogether still for a long while, before he breathed, 'You mean you don't care if they win?'

'I mean that we'll have to face facts . . . if they win,' I said. 'We'll have to adapt, in order to conserve as much as we can. We could be useful to them.'

That was when he hit me.

Well, I didn't hit back. I walked straight out of there, into the obscenely beautiful sunlight, and left him weeping. The next day we said nothing about the incident and worked together with stiff politeness.

But he has testified that I want to be a collaborationist.

Alice, did you ever understand what the war was about? You said goodbye with a gallantry which was almost more than I could endure, and the one time in these five years that I have had Earth furlough, we had too much else CENSOR CENSOR CENSOR. But I suspect that to you these imperial questions were simply a thing, like sickness or a floater crash, which could eat your man.

It was raining when last I left. The ground was still dark with winter, here and there a bank of dirty snow melting away. The sky hung low, like some vague grey roof, and threw tendrils of mist round the house. But I could see quite a distance across this ranch of ours, over the high plateau until the buttes, where I was someday going to take my son hunting, blocked off vision. The rain was soft, it made little drops in your hair, like Hiddy's blood – No, anyhow, I heard our brook chuckle, the one we installed the first year we owned the place, and the air smelled wet too, and I was as conscious of an aching toe as I was of your body of the stiffness in my gullet.

I hope you find yourself another man. That may not be easy. It won't be, if I know you; for you are a traitor's widow, and you have too much cleanliness to take one of those Brothers who will come sucking around. But, well, someone from the Cosmocorps, returning to cope as best he can with an Earth gone strange.

Sure, I'm jealous of him. But curiously, not of the fact that you will tell him, 'I love you' in the dark. Only of his becoming father to Jeanne and Bobby. So does this justify (Drusilla and others, now and then) when I never doubted you would stay loyal to me?

But I am supposed to justify something allegedly more important. The trouble is, it's so childishly simple that I can't see why this psychograph is needed.

Look! The Morwain and the Terrestrial spheres had interpenetrated long before the war. 'Border dispute' is a bad phrase; the universe is too big for borders. They have a thriving colony on the second planet of GGC 421387, which has extended its industry throughout the system. And this planet is a bare fifty light-years from Earth.

The fighting began much farther away. Savamor, as we call the planet in question – human throats can't make that particular music – was then a liability to them. They had to defend it, which tied up considerable strength.

We evacuated Asphodel, didn't we? Yes, but Savamor was too valuable. Not just the industry and the strategic location, though naturally they counted too. Savamor is a myth.

I have been there. That was as a newly fledged lieutenant, aboard the old *Danno-ura*, in days when the Fleet made goodwill visits. Already there were disputes, there had been clashes, an ugliness was in the air. We knew, and they knew, that we orbiting our ships around the planet as a warning.

Nevertheless we were understandably excited about getting leave. This was where the Dancers had gone to escape the upheavals at home, this was where they had raised those cities which remain a wonder and written the Declaration for a new chapter – oh, think of America shining before weary old Europe, but think also of Paris.

We got off at Darway port, and I shook my party in order to drift about on my own. When I was among elfin green towers, on a green-carpeted lane, and the long line of jewelposts glistened before me . . . what could I do but call it the Emerald City? After some hours I was tired and sat down on a terrace to hear the melodies. They're plangent, on no scale that men ever invented, but I liked them. Watching the beings go by, not just Morwain but beings from twenty different species, a thousand different cultures, I felt so cosmopolitan that it was like kissing my first girl.

Before long a Morwa joined me. 'Sir,' he said in fluent Esperanto – I won't try to remember the nuances of his accent – 'may this one have the joy of your presence?'

'My pleasure,' I said. And we got to talking. Of course, there was no drink, but none was required, I was quite intoxicated enough.

Tamulan was one of his names. At first we just exchanged pleasantries, then we got on to customs, then into politics. He was unfailing courteous, even when I got a little overheated about aggressions against our colonies. He simply pointed out how the matter looked from his side – but never mind now. You will be hearing the same things in years to come.

'We must not fight,' he said. 'We have too much in common.'

'Maybe that's why we do fight,' I said, and congratulated myself on so neat an insight.

His tentacles drooped; a man would have sighed. 'Perhaps so. But we are natural allies. Consider our societies, consider how the stars lie in the galaxy. Who would profit from a war between Earth and Morwai, except the Bilturs?'

In those days the Bilturs were remote from Sol. We hadn't borne their pressure, that had been Morwai's job. 'They're sentient too,' I said.

'They are monsters,' he replied. At the time, I didn't believe what he went on to tell me. Now I have studied too much to disbelieve. I will not admit that there is any race which has forfeited its right to existence, but there are certainly cultures which have.

'Come, though,' he said at length, 'twilight cools inward and

54

one hears a rustle of nest-bound feathers. Will you grace our home by taking dinner?'

Our home, you note. Not his, but his and his mates' and the fuzzy little cubs'. We can learn some things from the Morwain.

And they from us, to be sure. Chiaroscuro painting; Périgordian cuisine; the Bill of Rights. However, such matters have been cheapened by noise about What We Are Fighting For. They will need time to recover.

So what have we been fighting for? Not a few planets; both sides are realistic enough to horse trade them, albeit our conflicting claims were the proximate cause of battle. Nor, in truth, any desire on either side to impose a particular set of values on the galaxy; only our commentators are sufficiently stupid to believe that's even desirable. Why, then?

Why me? Why have I fought?

Because I was a career officer. Because men of my blood were fighting. Because I do not want aliens walking our land and ordering us about. *I do not.*

I say into the psychograph, and I am going to leave this tape unwiped because I most passionately want to be believed, my wish is that Earth should win. For this I would not only give my own life; that's easy, if you don't stop to think about the implications, and it's always possible. No, I would throw Alice, and Bobby, and Jeanne who must by now have become the most enchanting awkward hybrid of child and girl, into the furnace. Not to speak of Paris, and the caves where my ancestors drew the mammoths they dared hunt, and the whole damned state of Wyoming – from which it follows that Savamor planet would occasion me simply the mildest regret. Doesn't it?

As for why my feelings run thus, we must go deeper than psychodynamics has yet managed. In spite of glib talk about 'instinct of territoriality' and 'symbol of identification', I don't believe we really know

> *Why men were born: but surely we are brave,*
> *Who take the Golden Road to Samarkand.*

(Will they remember Flecker, when Earth has been changed?)

I'm rambling again. My position can be put approximately, in crude terms: Somebody has to have the final say – not any dictatorship, just the tribunal power – as to what is to happen in the galaxy. I want it to be my people.

No, let's modify that. I only want my people to have the final say as to what is to happen to them.

If, for this purpose, we must destroy Tamulan who was so hospitable, and his mates and his fuzzy cubs that climbed over my knees, and the Emerald City, well, so be it. Earth should not be dominated by anyone. Nor dominate anyone else, ideally; trouble is, nobody's allowed simply to mind his own business. We get down to some kind of bedrock when we say that man must be free to settle man's destiny.

My question, then, is merely, What do you do when you see that this isn't going to be possible?

I would like to write a love letter to Earth, but I am no writer and I can only call up a jumble: a sky that burned with sunset one snow-clad evening; 'We hold these truths to be self-evident, that all men are created free and equal;' the astonishing smallness of Stonehenge, so that you need some time to feel the sheer mass of it, and the astonishing mass of the Parthenon, so that you must sit a while in the spilling Athenian sunlight to grasp its beauty; moonlight on a restless ocean; Beethoven's quartets; the cadence of boots in a rain-wet street; a hand axe chipped out by some heavy-browed Neanderthal who also wondered why men were born; a kiss which becomes more than a kiss, and nine months later a red, wrinkled, indignant blob of life; the feel of a horse's muscles flowing between my thighs; caviar, champagne, and eyes meeting in the middle of elegance; outrageous puns; Mrs Elton, my neighbour, who raised three sons to manhood after her own man was dead – no, the clock is moving. I have to compose my thoughts most carefully now.

None less than General Wang briefed me. He sat in the command room, in the depths of Hell-Won't-Have-It, with the star tank a-glitter behind his big bald head, and after I came to attention there was a silence so long that the rustle of the ventilators began to run up and down my spine. When he finally said, 'At ease, Colonel. Sit down,' I was shocked to hear he had grown old.

He played with a duplipen for a while longer before he raised his eyes and said: 'You notice we are alone. This is a matter for absolute security. At present an 87 per cent probability of success is computed – success defined as mission accomplished with less than 50 per cent casualties – but if word should get out the operation will become hopeless.'

I never really believed those rumours about Morwain agents among us. No being who would sell out his own species could make officer grade, could he? However, I nodded, and said, 'Understood, sir.'

He swivelled around to face the tank. 'This thing has a very limited value,' he remarked in the same dead voice. 'There are too many stars. But it can illustrate the present situation. Observe.' His hands passed over the controls, some of those swimming points of light turned gold and some blood colour.

Enemy colour.

I saw how we had reeled back across the parsecs, I saw the ugly salient thrusting in among those suns which still were ours, and even then I guessed what was to come and snatched after words of protest.

'This system . . . entire sector dependent on it . . . interior lines of communication . . . depots . . . repair centre – ' I scarcely heard. I was back on Savamor, in Tamulan's home.

Oh, yes, a squadron could get through. Space is too big to guard everywhere. One would meet defences at the end of the trip, which were not too heavy when attack was unexpected, and afterward one must fight back through ships which would converge like hornets from every point of the three-diminsional compass; but yes, indeed, the probability was more than 85 per cent that one could shoot a doomsday barrage into the sky of Savamor.

It wouldn't even be inhumane. Simply a concerted flash of so many megatons that the whole atmosphere was turned momentarily into an incandescent plasma. True, the firestorms would run for months afterward, and nothing would be left but desert, and if any life whatsoever survived it would need several million years to crawl back from the oceans. But Tamulan would never know what had happened. If Tamulan wasn't off with his own fleet somewhere; if he hadn't already died with a laser beam through his guts, or gasping for air that wasn't around him any longer, or vomiting in radiation sickness, as I'd seen human men do. Without a habitable planet for their economic foundation, industries on the other worlds around GGC 421387 could no longer be maintained. Without the entire system for base and supply centre, the salient must be pinched off. Without that salient, pointed like a knife at Earth –

'Sir,' I said, 'they haven't bombarded any of our colonies.'

'Nor we any of theirs,' Wang said. 'Now we have no choice.'

57

'But – '

'Be still!' He surged half out of his chair. One eyelid began to twitch. 'Do you think I have not lain awake about this?'

Presently, in the monotone with which he began: 'It will be a heavy setback for them. We will be able to hold this sector for an estimated year longer: which is to say, prolong the war a year.'

'For the sake of that – '

'Much could happen in a year. We might develop a new weapon. They might decide Earth is too expensive a conquest. If nothing else, a year can be lived in, back home.'

'Suppose they retaliate,' I said.

He is a brave man; he met my gaze. 'One cannot act, or even exist, without risk,' he said.

I had no answer.

'If you feel grave objections, Colonel,' he said, 'I shall not order you into this. I shall not so much as think ill of you. There are plenty of others.'

Nor could I answer that.

Be it made plain here, as it was at my eminently fair trial: no man under my command is in any way to blame for what happened. Our squadron took space with myself the only one in all those ships who knew what the mission was. My subordinate captains had been told about a raid in the Savamor environ, and took for granted that we were after some rogue planet used for a stronghold, much like our own. The missile officers must have had their suspicions, after noting what cargo was given into their care, but they stand far down the chain. And they assumed that last-minute information caused me to shift course and make for Cantrell's Cluster. There we fought our bloody, valiant, and altogether futile battle, won, and limped home again.

Thus I am responsible for much death and maiming. Why?

My official defence was that I had decided the attack on Savamor was lunacy, but knowing that the Morwain salient also depended on the Cluster, I hoped to accomplish our purpose by a surprise attack there. Nonsense. We only shook them up a little, as any second-year cadet could have predicted.

My private reason is that I had to cripple the strength which Wang would otherwise use to destroy Savamor, with a more reliable officer in charge. Facts vindicate my logic. We have already abandoned Hell-Won't-Have-It, and could now find no way past the triumphantly advancing enemy. Nor would there be any point in it; they have straightened out their front and the rest of the war must be fought along conventional lines.

My ultimate motive was the hope of being captured. They would have treated us decently, as we have thus far treated our own prisoners. In time I would have returned to Alice, with the favour of the Morwain behind me. And isn't my race going to need go-betweens?

Eventually, leaders? For they can't hold us down too long. The Bilturs are coming, the Morwain will want allies. We can set a price on our friendship, and the price can perhaps be freedom.

Once upon a time, the English fought the French, and the Americans fought the English, and those were fairly clean wars as wars go. They left no lasting hates. It was possible later for the nations to make fellowship in the face of the real enemy. But who, across the centuries, has forgiven Dachau?

Had we fired on Savamor, I don't believe the Morwain would have laid Earth waste. Tamulan's people aren't that kind. Nevertheless, would they not have felt bound to tear down every work, every institution, every dream of the race which was capable of such a thing, and rebuild in their own image? And could they ever have trusted us again?

Whereas, having fought and been defeated honourably, we may hope to save what is really ours: may even hope to have it admired and imitated, a decade or two from now.

Of course, this is predicated on the assumption that Earth will lose the war. One keeps believing a miracle will come, can we but hold out long enough. I did myself; I had to strangle the belief. And then, in my arrogance, I set my single judgment against what can only be called that of my entire people.

Was I right? Will my statue stand beside Jefferson's and Lincoln's, for Bobby to point at and say, He was my father – ? Or will they spit on our name until he must change it in the silly hope of vanishing? I don't know. I never will.

So I am now going to spend what time remains in thinking about

THE DIPTEROID
PHENOMENON

Moru understood about guns. At least, the tall strangers had demonstrated to their guides what the things that each of them carried at his hip could do in a flash and a flameburst. But he did not realize that the small objects they often moved about in their hands, while talking in their own language, were audiovisual transmitters. Probably he thought they were fetishes.

Thus, when he killed Donli Sairn, he did so in full view of Donli's wife.

That was happenstance. Except for prearranged times, morning and evening of the planet's twenty-eight hour day, the biologist, like his fellows, sent only to his computer. But because they had not been married long, and were helplessly happy, Evalyth received his 'casts whenever she could get away from her own duties.

The coincidence that she was tuned in at that one moment was not great. There was little for her to do. As militech of the expedition – she being from a half barbaric part of Kraken where the sexes had equal opportunities to learn of combat suitable to primitive environments – she had overseen the building of a compound; and she kept the routines of guarding it under a close eye. However, the inhabitants of Lokon were as co-operative with the visitors from heaven as mutual mysteriousness allowed. Every instinct and experience assured Evalyth Sairn that their reticence masked nothing except awe, with perhaps a wistful hope of friendship. Captain Jonafer agreed. Her position having thus become rather a sinecure, she was trying to learn enough about Donli's work to be a useful assistant after he returned from the lowlands.

Also, a medical test had lately confirmed that she was pregnant. She wouldn't tell him, she decided: not yet, over all those hundreds of kilometres, but when they lay again together. Meanwhile, the knowledge that they had begun a new life made him a lodestar to her.

On the afternoon of his death she entered the biolab whistling. Outside, sunlight struck fierce and brass-coloured on dusty ground, on prefab shacks huddled about the boat which had brought everyone and everything down from the orbit where *New Dawn* circled, on the parked flitters and gravsleds that took men around the big island that was the only habitable land on this globe, on the men and the women themselves. Beyond the stockade, plumy treetops, a glimpse of mud-brick buildings, a murmur of voices and mutter of footfalls, a drift of bitter woodsmoke, showed that a town of several thousand people sprawled between here and Lake Zelo.

The biolab occupied more than half the structure where the Sairns lived. Comforts were few, when ships from a handful of cultures struggling back to civilization ranged across the ruins of empire. For Evalyth, though, it sufficed that this was their home. She was used to austerity anyway. One thing that had first attracted her to Donli, meeting him on Kraken, was the cheerfulness with which he, a man from Atheia, which was supposed to have retained or regained almost as many amenities as Old Earth knew in its glory, had accepted life in her gaunt grim country.

The gravity field here was 0.77 standard, less than two-thirds of what she had grown up in. Her gait was easy through the clutter of apparatus and specimens. She was a big young woman, good-looking in the body, a shade too strong in the features for most men's taste outside her own folk. She had their blondness and, on legs and forearms, their intricate tattoos; the blaster at her waist had come down through many generations. Otherwise she had abandoned Krakener costume for the plain coveralls of the expedition.

How cool and dim the shack was! She sighed with pleasure, sat down and activated the receiver. As the image formed, three-dimensional in the air, and Donli's voice spoke, her heart sprang a little.

' – appears to be descending from a clover.'

The image was of plants with green trilobate leaves, scattered low among the reddish native pseudo-grasses. It swelled as Donli brought the transmitter near, so that the computer might record details for later analysis. Evalyth frowned, trying to recall what . . . oh, yes. Clover was another of those life forms that man had brought with him from Old Earth, to more planets than anyone now remembered, before the Long Night fell. Often they were virtually unrecognizable; over thousands of years, evolution had fitted them to alien conditions, or mutation and genetic drift had acted on small initial populations in a nearly random fashion. No one on Kraken had known that pines and gulls and rhizobacteria were altered immigrants, until Donli's crew arrived and identified them. Not that he, or anybody from this part of the galaxy, had yet made it back to the mother world. But the Atheian data banks were packed with information, and so was Donli's dear curly head –

And there was his hand, huge in the field of view, gathering specimens. She wanted to kiss it. *Patience, patience,* the officer part of her reminded the bride. *We're here to work. We've discovered one more lost colony, the most wretched one so far, sunken back to utter primitivism. Our duty is to advise the Board whether a civilizing mission is worthwhile, or whether the slender resources that the Allied Planets can spare had better be used elsewhere, leaving these people in their misery for another two or three hundred years. To make an honest report, we must study them, their cultures, their world. That's why I'm in the barbarian highlands and he's down in the jungle among out-and-out savages.*

Please finish soon, darling.

She heard Donli speak in the lowland dialect. It was a debased form of Lokonese, which in turn was remotely descended from Anglic. The expedition's linguists had unravelled the language in a few intensive weeks. Then all personnel took a brain-feed in it. Nonetheless, she admired how quickly her man had become fluent in the woodsrunners' version, after mere days of conversation with them.

'Are we not coming to the place, Moru? You said the thing was close by our camp.'

'We are nearly arrived, man-from-the-clouds.'

A tiny alarm struck within Evalyth. What was going on? Donli hadn't left his companions to strike off alone with a native, had he? Rogar of Lokon had warned them to beware of treachery on those parts. But, to be sure, only yesterday the guides had rescued Haimie Fiell when he tumbled into a swift-running river . . . at some risk to themselves . . .

The view bobbed as the transmitter swung in Donli's grasp. It made Evalyth a bit dizzy. From time to time she got glimpses of the broader setting. Forest crowded about a game trail, rust-coloured leafage, brown trunks and branches, shadows beyond, the occasional harsh call of something unseen. She could practically feel the heat and dank weight of the atmosphere, smell the unpleasant pungencies. This world (which no longer had a name, except World, because the dwellers upon it had forgotten what the stars really were) was ill suited to colonization. The life it had spawned was often poisonous, always nutritionally deficient. With the help of species they had brought along, men survived marginally. The original settlers doubtless meant to improve matters. But then the breakdown came – evidence was that their single town had been missiled out of existence, a majority of the people with it – and resources were lacking to rebuild, and the miracle was that anything human remained except bones.

'Now, here, man-from-the-clouds.'

The swaying scene grew steadily. Silence hummed from jungle to cabin. 'I do not see anything,' Donli said at length.

'Follow me. I show.'

Donli put his transmitter in the fork of a tree. It scanned him and Moru while they moved across a meadow. The guide looked childish beside the space traveller, barely up to his shoulder: an old child, though, near-naked body seamed with scars and lame in the right foot from some injury of the past, face wizened in a great black bush of hair and beard. He, who could not hunt, could only fish and trap to support his family, was even more impoverished than his fellows. He must have been happy indeed when the flitter landed near their village and the strangers offered fabulous trade goods for a week or two of being shown around the countryside. Donli had projected the image of Moru's straw hut for Evalyth, the pitiful few possessions, the woman already worn out with toil, the two surviving sons who, at ages said to be about seven or eight, which would equal twelve or thirteen standard years, were shrivelled gnomes.

Roger had seemed to declare – the Lokonese tongue was by no means perfectly understood yet – that the lowlanders would be less poor if they weren't such a vicious lot, tribe forever at war with tribe. *But really*, Evalyth thought, *what possible menace can they be?*

63

Moru's gear consisted of a loinstrap, a cord around his body for preparing snares, an obsidian knife, and a knapsack so woven and greased that it could hold liquids at need. The other men of his group, being able to pursue game and to win a share of booty by taking part in battles, were noticeably better off. They didn't look much different in person, however, Without room for expansion, the island populace must be highly inbred.

The dwarfish man squatted, parting a shrub with his hands. 'Here,' he grunted, and stood up again.

Evalyth knew well the eagerness that kindled in Donli. Nevertheless he turned around, smiled straight into the transmitter, and said in Atheian: 'Maybe you're watching, dearest, If so, I'd like to share this with you. It may be a bird's nest.'

She remembered vaguely that the existence of birds would be an ecologically significant datum. What mattered was what he had just said to her. 'Oh yes, oh yes!' she wanted to cry. But his group had only two receivers with them, and he wasn't carrying either.

She saw him kneel in the long ill-coloured vegetation. She saw him reach with the gentleness she also knew, into the shrub, easing its branches aside, holding his breath lest he –

She saw Moru leap upon his back. The savage wrapped legs about Donli's middle. His left hand seized Donli's hair and pulled the head back. The knife flew back in his right.

Blood spurted from beneath Donli's jaw. He couldn't shout, not with his throat gaping open, he could only bubble and croak while Moru haggled the wound wider. He reached blindly for his gun. Moru dropped the knife and caught his arms, they rolled over in that embrace, Donli threshed and flopped in the spouting of his own blood, Moru hung on, the brush trembled around them and hid them, until Moru rose red and dripping, painted, panting, and Evalyth screamed into the transmitter beside her, into the universe, and she kept on screaming and fought them when they tried to take her away from the scene in the meadow where Moru went about his butcher's work, until something stung her with coolness and she toppled into the bottom of the universe whose stars had all gone out forever.

Haimie Fiell said through white lips: 'No, of course we didn't know till you alerted us. He and that – creature – were several kilometres from our camp. *Why* didn't you let us go after him right away?'

'Because of what we'd seen on the transmission,' Captain Jonafer replied. 'Sairn was irretrievably dead. You could've been ambushed, arrows in the back or something, pushing down those narrow trails. Best you stay where you were, guarding each other, till we got a vehicle to you.'

Fiell looked past the big grey-haired man, out of the door of the command hut, to the stockade and the unpitying noon sky. 'But what that little monster was doing meanwhile –' Abruptly he closed his mouth.

With equal haste, Jonafer said: 'The other guides ran away, you've told me, as soon as they sensed you were angry. I've just had a report from Kallaman. His team flitted to the village. It's deserted. The whole tribe's pulled up stakes. Afraid of our revenge, evidently. Though it's no large chore to move, when you can carry your household goods on your back and weave yourself a new house in a day.'

Evalyth leaned forward. 'Stop evading me,' she said. 'What did Moru do with Donli that you might have prevented if you'd arrived in time?'

Fiell continued to look past her. Sweat gleamed in droplets on his forehead. 'Nothing, really,' he mumbled. 'Nothing that mattered . . . once the murder itself had been committed.'

'I meant to ask you what kind of services you want for him, Lieutenant Sairn,' Jonafer said to her. 'Should the ashes be buried here, or scattered in space after we leave, or brought home?'

Evalyth turned her gaze full upon him. 'I never authorized that he be cremated, Captain,' she said slowly.

'No, but – Well, be realistic. You were first under anaesthesia, then heavy sedation, while we recovered the body. Time had passed. We've no facilities for, um, cosmetic repair, nor any extra refrigeration space, and in this heat –'

Since she had been let out of sickbay, there had been a kind of numbness in Evalyth. She could not entirely comprehend the fact that Donli was gone. It seemed as if at any instant yonder doorway would fill with him, sunlight across his shoulders, and he would call to her, laughing, and console her for a meaningless nightmare she had had. That was the effect of the psychodrugs, she knew, and damned the kindliness of the medic.

She was almost glad to feel a slow rising of anger. It meant the drugs were wearing off. By evening she would be able to weep.

'Captain,' she said, 'I saw him killed. I've seen deaths before, some of them quite as messy. We don't mask the truth on Kraken.

You've cheated me of my right to lay my man out and close his eyes. You will not cheat me of my right to obtain justice. I demand to know exactly what happened.'

Jonafer's fists knotted on his desktop. 'I can hardly stand to tell you.'

'But you shall, Captain.'

'All right! All right!' Jonafer shouted. The words leaped out like bullets. 'We saw the thing transmitted. He stripped Donli, hung him up by the heels from a tree, bled him into that knapsack. He cut off the genitals and threw them in with the blood. He opened the body and took heart, lungs, liver, kidneys, thyroid, prostate, pancreas, and loaded them up too, and ran off into the woods. Do you wonder why we didn't let you see what was left?'

'The Lokonese warned us against the jungle dwellers,' Fiell said dully. 'We should have listened. But they seemed like pathetic dwarfs. And they did rescue me from the river. When Donli asked about birds – described them, you know, and asked if anything like that was known – Moru said yes, but they were rare and shy; our gang would scare them off; but if one man would come along with him, he could find a nest and they might see the bird. 'A "house", he called it, but Donli thought he meant a nest. Or so he told us. It'd been a talk with Moru when they happened to be a ways offside, in sight but out of earshot. Maybe that should have alerted us, maybe we should have asked the other tribesmen. But we didn't see any reason to – I mean. Donli was bigger, stronger, armed with a blaster, what savage would dare attack him, and anyway, they *had* been friendly, downright frolicsome after they got over their initial fear of us, and they'd shown as much eagerness for further contact as anybody here in Lokon has, and –' His voice trailed off.

'Did he steal tools or weapons?' Evalyth asked.

'No,' Jonafer said. 'I have everything your husband was carrying, ready to give you.'

Fiell said: 'I don't think it was an act of hatred. Moru must have had some superstitious reason.'

Jonafer nodded. 'We can't judge him by our standards.'

'By whose, then?' Evalyth retorted. Supertranquillizer or no, she was surprised at the evenness of her own tone. 'I'm from Kraken, remember. I'll not let Donli's child be born and grow up knowing he was murdered and no one tried to get justice for him.'

'You can't take revenge on an entire tribe,' Jonafer said.

'I don't mean to. But – Captain, the personnel of this expedition are from several different planets, each with its characteristic societies. The articles specifically state that the essential mores of every member shall be respected. I want to be relieved of my regular duties until I have arrested the killer of my husband and done justice upon him.'

Jonafer bent his head. 'I have to grant that,' he said low.

Evalyth rose. 'Thank you, gentlemen,' she said. 'If you will excuse me, I'll commence my investigation at once.'

– while she was still a machine, before the drugs wore off.

In the drier, cooler uplands, agriculture had remained possible after the colony otherwise lost civilization. Fields and orchards, painstakingly cultivated with neolithic tools, supported a scattering of villages and the capital town Lokon.

Its people bore a family resemblance to the forest dwellers. Few settlers indeed could have survived to become the ancestors of this world's humanity. But the highlanders were better nourished, bigger, straighter. They wore gaily dyed tunics and sandals. The well-to-do added jewellery of gold and silver. Hair was braided, chins kept shaven. Folk walked boldy, without the savages' constant fear of ambush, and talked merrily.

To be sure, this was only strictly true of the free. While *New Dawn*'s anthropologists had scarcely begun to unravel the ins and outs of the culture, it had been obvious from the first that Lokon kept a large slave class. Some were sleek household servants. More toiled meek and naked in the fields, the quarries, the mines, under the lash of overseers and the guard of soldiers whose spearheads and swords were of ancient Imperial metal. But none of the space travellers were unduly shocked. They had seen worse elsewhere. Historical data banks described places in olden time called Athens, India, America.

Evalyth strode down twisted, dusty streets, between the gaudily painted walls of cubical, windowless adobe houses. Commoners going about their tasks made respectful salutes. Although no one feared any longer that the strangers meant harm, she did tower above the tallest man, her hair was coloured like metal and her eyes like the sky, she bore lightning at her waist and none knew what other godlike powers.

Today soldiers and noblemen also genuflected while slaves went on their faces. Where she appeared, the chatter and clatter of everyday life vanished; the business of the market plaza halted when she passed the booths; children ceased their games and fled; she moved in a silence akin to the silence in her soul. Under the sun and the snowcone of Mount Burus, horror brooded. For by now Lokon knew that a man from the stars had been slain by a lowland brute; and what would come of that?

Word must have gone ahead to Rogar, though, since he awaited her in his house by Lake Zelo next to the Sacred Place. He was not king or council president or high priest, but he was something of all three, and he it was who dealt most with the strangers.

His dwelling was the usual kind, larger than average but dwarfed by the adjacent walls. Those enclosed a huge compound, filled with buildings, where none of the outworlders had been admitted. Guards in scarlet robes and grotesquely carved wooden helmets stood always at its gates. Today their numbers were doubled, and others flanked Rogar's door. The lake shone like polished steel at their backs. The trees along the shore looked equally rigid.

Rogar's majordomo, a fat elderly slave, prostrated himself in the entrance as Evalyth neared. 'If the heaven-borne will deign to follow this unworthy one, *Klev* Rogar is within – ' The guards dipped their spears to her. Their eyes were wide and frightened.

Like the other houses, this turned inward. Rogar sat on a dais in a room opening on a courtyard. It seemed doubly cool and dim by contrast with the glare outside. She could scarcely discern the frescos on the walls or the patterns on the carpet; they were crude art anyway. Her attention focused on Rogar. He did not rise, that not being a sign of respect here. Instead, he bowed his grizzled head above folded hands. The major-domo offered her a bench and Rogar's chief wife set a bombilla of herb tea by her before vanishing into the women's quarters.

'Be greeted, *Klev*,' Evalyth said formally.

'Be greeted, heaven-borne.' Alone now, shadowed from the cruel sun, they observed a ritual period of silence.

Then: 'This is terrible what has happened, heaven-born,' Rogar said. 'Perhaps you do not know that my white robe and bare feet signify mourning as for one of my own blood.'

'That is well done,' Evalyth said. 'We shall remember.'

The man's dignity faltered. 'You understand that none of us have anything to do with the evil, do you not? The savages are our enemies too. They are vermin. Our ancestors caught some and made them slaves, but they are good for nothing else. I warned your friends not to go down among those we have not tamed.'

'Their wish was to do so,' Evalyth replied. 'Now my wish is to get revenge for my man.' She didn't know if this language included a word for justice. No matter. Because of the drugs, which heightened the logical faculties while they muffled the emotions, she was speaking Lokonese quite well enough for her purposes.

'We can gather soldiers and help you kill as many as you choose,' Rogar offered.

'Not needful. With this weapon at my side I alone can destroy more than your army might. I want your counsel and help in a different matter. How can I find him who slew my man?'

Rogar frowned. 'The savages can vanish into trackless jungles, heaven-borne.'

'Can they vanish from other savages, though?'

'Ah! Shrewdly thought, heaven-borne. Those tribes are endlessly at each other's throats. If we can make contact with one, its hunters will soon learn for you where the killer's people have taken themselves.' His scowl deepened. 'But he may have gone from them, to hide until you have departed our land. A single man might be impossible to find. Lowlanders are good at hiding, of necessity.'

'What do you mean by necessity?'

Rogar showed surprise at her failure to grasp what was obvious to him. 'Why, consider a man out hunting,' he said. 'He cannot go with companions after every kind of game, or the noise and scent would frighten it away. So he is often alone in the jungle. Someone from another tribe may well set upon him. A man stalked and killed is just as useful as one slain in open war.'

'Why this incessant fighting?'

Rogar's look of bafflement grew stronger. 'How else shall they get human flesh?'

'But they do not live on that!'

'No, surely not, except as needed. But that need comes many times, as you know. Their wars are their chief way of taking men; booty is good too, but not the main reason to fight. He who slays, owns the corpse, and naturally divides it solely among his close kin. Not everyone is lucky in battle. Therefore those who did not chance to kill in a war may well go hunting on their own, two or three of them together hoping to find a single man from a different tribe. And that is why a lowlander must be skilful at hiding.'

Evalyth did not move or speak. Rogar drew a long breath and continued trying to explain: 'Heaven-borne, when I heard the evil news, I spoke long with men from your company. They told me what they had seen from afar by the wonderful means you command. Thus it is clear to me what happened. This guide, what is his name, yes, Moru, he is a cripple. He had no hope of killing himself a man except by treachery. When he saw that chance he took it.'

He ventured a smile. 'That would never happen in the highlands,' he declared. 'We do not fight wars, save when we are attacked, nor do we hunt our fellow men as if they were animals. Like yours, ours is a civilized race.' His lips drew back from startlingly white teeth. 'But heaven-borne, your man was slain. I propose we take vengeance, not simply on the killer if we catch him, but on his tribe, which we can certainly find as you suggested. That will teach all the savages to beware of their betters. Afterwards we can share the flesh, half to your people, half to mine.'

Evalyth could only know an intellectual astonishment. Yet she had the feeling somehow of having walked off a cliff. She stared through the shadows, into the grave old face, and after a long she heard herself whisper: 'You . . . also . . . here . . . eat men?'

'Slaves,' Rogar said. 'No more than required. One of them will do for four boys.'

Her hand dropped to her gun. Rogar sprang up in alarm. 'Heaven-borne,' he exclaimed, 'I told you we are civilized! Never fear attack from any of us! We – we –'

She rose too, high above him. Did he read judgement in her gaze? Was the terror that snatched him on behalf of his whole people? He cowered from her, sweating and shuddering. 'Heaven-borne, believe me, you have no quarrel with Lokon – no, now, let me show you, let me take you into the Sacred Place, even if, if you are no initiate . . . for surely you are akin to the gods, surely the gods will not be offended – Come, let me show you how it is, let me prove we have no will and no *need* to be your enemies –'

There was the gate that Rogar opened for her in that massive wall. There were the shocked countenances of the guards and loud promises of many sacrifices to appease the Powers. There was a stone pavement beyond, hot and hollowly resounding underfoot. There were the idols grinning around the central temple. There was the house of the acolytes who did the work and who shrank in fear when they saw their master conduct a foreigner in. There were the slave barracks.

'See, heaven-borne, they are well-treated are they not? We do have to crush their hands and feet when we choose them as children for this service. Think how dangerous it would be otherwise, hundreds of boys and young men in here. But we treat them kindly unless they misbehave. Are they not fat? Their own Holy Food is especially honourable, bodies of men of all degree who have died in their full strength. We teach them that they will live on in those for whom they are slain. Most are content with that, believe me, heaven-borne. Ask them yourself . . . though remember, they grow dull-witted, with nothing to do year after year. We slay them quickly, cleanly, at the beginning of each summer – no more than we must for that year's crop of boys entering into manhood, one slave for four boys, no more than that. And it is a most beautiful rite with days of feasting and merrymaking afterwards. Do you understand now, heaven-borne? You have nothing to fear from us. We are not savages, warring and raiding and skulking to get our man-flesh. We are civilized – not godlike in your fashion, no, I dare not claim that, do not be angry – but civilized – surely worthy of your friendship, are we not, are we not, heaven-borne?'

Chena Darnard, who headed the cultural anthropology team told her computer to scan its data bank. Like the others, it was portable, its memory housed in *New Darwin*. At the moment the spaceship was above the opposite hemisphere, and perceptible time passed while beams went back and forth along the strung-out relay units.

Chena leaned back and studied Evalyth across her desk. The Krakener girl sat so quietly. It seemed unnatural, despite the drugs in her bloodstream retaining some power. To be sure, Evalyth was of aristocratic descent in a warlike society. Furthermore, heredity psychological as well as physiological differences might exist on the different worlds. Not much was known about that, apart from extreme cases like Gwydion (or this planet?). Regardless, Chena thought it would be better if Evalyth gave way to simple shock and grief.

'Are you quite certain of your facts, dear?' the anthropologist asked as gently as possible. 'I mean, while this island alone is habitable, it's large, the topography is rugged, communications

71

are primitive, my group has already identified scores of distinct cultures.'

'I questioned Rogar for more than an hour,' Evalyth replied in the same flat voice, as before. 'I know interrogation techniques, and he was badly rattled. He talked.

'The Lokonese themselves are not as backward as their technology. They've lived for centuries with savages threatening their borderlands. It's made them develop a good intelligence network. Rogar described its functioning to me in detail. It can't help but keep them reasonably well-informed about everything that goes on. And, while tribal customs do vary tremendously, the cannibalism is universal. That's why none of the Lokonese thought to mention it to us. They took for granted that we had our own ways of providing human meat.'

'People have, m-m-m, latitude in those methods?'

'Oh yes. Here they breed slaves for the purpose. But most low-landers have too skimpy an economy for that. Some of them use war and murder. Among others, men past a certain age draw lots for who shall die. Among still others, they settle it within the tribe by annual combats. Or – Who cares? The fact is that, everywhere in this country, in whatever fashion it may be, the boys undergo a puberty rite that involves eating an adult male.'

Chena bit her lip. 'What in the name of chaos might have started – ? Computer! Have you scanned?'

'Yes,' said the machine voice out of the case on her desk. 'Data on cannibalism in man are comparatively sparse, because it is a rarity. On all planets hitherto known to us it is banned, and has been throughout their history, although it is sometimes considered forgivable as an emergency measure when no alternative means of preserving life is available. Very limited forms of what be called ceremonial cannibalism have occurred, as for example the drinking of minute amounts of each other's blood in pledging oath brotherhood among the Falkems of Lochlanna –'

'Never mind that,' Chena said. A tautness in her throat thickened her tone. 'Only here, it seems, have they degenerated so far that – Or is it degeneracy? Reversion, perhaps? What about Old Earth?'

'Information is fragmentary. Aside from what was lost during the Long Night, knowledge is under the handicap that the last primitive societies there vanished before interstellar travel began. But certain data collected by ancient historians and scientists remain.

'Cannibalism was an occasional part of human sacrifice. As a rule, victims were left uneaten. But in a minority of religions, the bodies, or selected portions of them, were consumed, either by a special class, or by the community as a whole. Generally this was regarded as theophagy. Thus, the Aztecs of Mexico offered thousands of individuals annually to their gods. The requirement of doing this forced them to provoke wars and rebellions, which in turn made it easy for the eventual European conqueror to get native allies. The majority of prisoners were simply slaughtered, their hearts given directly to the idols. But in at least one cult the body was divided among the worshippers.

'Cannibalism could be a form of magic, too. By eating a person, one supposedly acquired his virtues. This was the principal motive of the cannibals of Africa and Polynesia. Contemporary observers did report that the meals were relished, but that is easy to understand, especially in protein-poor areas.

'The sole recorded instance of systematic non-ceremonial cannibalism was among the Carib Indians of America. They ate man because they preferred man. They were especially fond of babies, and used to capture women from other tribes for breeding stock. Male children of these slaves were generally gelded to make them docile and tender. In large part because of strong aversion to such practices, the Europeans exterminated the Caribs to the last man.'

The report stopped. Chena grimaced. 'I can sympathize with the Europeans,' she said.

Evalyth might once have raised her eyebrows; but her face stayed as wooden as her speech. 'Aren't you supposed to be an objective scientist?'

'Yes. Yes. Still, there is such a thing as value judgement. And they did kill Donli.'

'Not they. One of them. I shall find him.'

'He's nothing but a creature of his culture, dear, sick with his whole race.' Chena drew a breath, struggling for calm. 'Obviously, the sickness has become a behavioural basic,' she said. 'I daresay it originated in Lokon. Cultural radiation is practically always from the more advanced peoples. And on a single island, after centuries, no tribe has escaped the infection. The Lokonese later elaborated and rationalized the practice. The savages left its cruelty naked. But highlander or lowlander, their way of life is founded on that particular human sacrifice.'

'Can't they be taught differently?' Evalyth asked without real interest.

'Yes. In time. In theory. But – well, I do know enough about what happened on Old Earth, and elsewhere, when advanced societies undertook to reform primitive ones. The entire structure was destroyed. It had to be.

'Think of the result, if we told these people to desist from their puberty rite. They wouldn't listen. They couldn't. They *must* have grandchildren. They *know* a boy won't become a man unless he has eaten part of a man. We'd have to conquer them, kill most, make sullen prisoners of the rest. And when the next crop of boys did in fact mature without the magic food . . . what then? Can you imagine the demoralization, the sense of utter inferiority, the loss of that tradition which is the core of every personal identity? It might be kinder to bomb this island sterile.'

Chena shook her head. 'No,' she said harshly, 'the single decent way for us to proceed would be gradually. We could send missionaries. By their precept and example, we could start the natives phasing out their custom after two or three generations. . . And we can't afford such an effort. Not for a long time to come. Not with so many other worlds in the glaxy, so much worthier of what little help we can give. I am going to recommend we depart as soon as possible. When we get home, I shall recommend this planet be left alone.'

Evalyth considered her for a moment before asking: 'Isn't that partly because of your own reaction?'

'Yes,' Chena admitted. 'I can't overcome my disgust. And I, as you pointed out, am supposed to be professionally broad-minded. So even if the Board tried to recruit missionaries, I doubt if they'd succeed.' She hesitated. 'You yourself, Evalyth –'

The Krakener rose. 'My emotions don't matter,' she said. 'My duty does. Thank you for your help.' She turned on her heel and went with military strides out of the cabin.

The chemical barriers were crumbling. Evalyth stood for a moment before the little building that had been hers and Donli's, afraid to enter. The sun was low, so that the compound was filling with shadows. A thing, leathery-winged and serpentine, cruised silently overhead. From outside the stockade drifted sounds of feet, foreign voices, the whine of a wooden flute. The air was cooling. She shivered. Their home would be too hollow.

Someone approached. She recognized the person glimpsewise,

Alsabeta Mondain from Nuevamerica. Listening to her well-meant foolish condolences would be worse than going inside. Evalyth took the last three steps and slid the door shut behind her.

Donli will not be here again. Eternally.

But the cabin proved not to be empty of him. Rather, it was too full. That chair where he used to sit, reading that worn volume of poetry which she could not understand and teased him about, that table across which he had toasted her and tossed kisses, that closet where his clothes hung, that scuffed pair of slippers, that bed, it screamed of him. Evalyth went fast into the laboratory section and drew the curtain that separated it from the living quarters. Rings rattled along the rod. The noise was monstrous in twilight.

She closed her eyes and fists and stood breathing hard. *I will not go soft*, she declared. *You always said you loved me for my strength (among numerous other desirable features, you'd add with your slow grin, but I won't remember that yet), and I don't aim to let slip anything you loved.*

I've got to get busy, she told Donli's child. *The expedition command is pretty sure to act on Chena's urging and haul mass for home. We've not many days to avenge your father.*

Her eyes snapped open. *What am I doing*, she thought, bewildered, *talking to a dead man and an embryo?*

She turned on the overhead fluoro and went to the computer. It was made no differently from the other portables. Donli had used it. But she could look away from the unique scratches and bumps on that square case, as she could not escape his microscope chemanalysers, chromosome tracer, biological specimens . . . She seated herself. A drink would have been very welcome, except that she needed clarity. 'Activate!' she ordered.

The On light glowed yellow. Evalyth tugged her chin, searching for words. 'The objective,' she said at length, 'is to trace a lowlander who has consumed several kilos of flesh and blood from one of the party, and afterwards vanished into the jungle. The killing took place about sixty hours ago. How can he be found?'

The least hum answered her. She imagined the links: to the maser in the ferry, up past the sky to the nearest orbiting relay unit, to the next, to the next, around the bloated belly of the planet, by ogre sun and unhuman stars, until the pulses reached the mother ship: then down to an unliving brain that routed the question to the appropriate data bank: then to the scanners, whose resonating energies flew from molecule to distorted molecule, identifying more bits of information than it made sense to number, data garnered from hundreds or thousands of entire worlds, data preserved through the wreck of Empire and the dark ages that followed, data going back to an Old Earth that perhaps no longer existed. She shied from the thought and wished herself back on dear stern Kraken. *We will go there*, she promised Donli's child. *You will dwell apart from these too many machines and grow up as the gods meant you should.*

'Query,' said the artificial voice. 'Of what origin was the victim of this assault?'

Evalyth must wet her lips before she could reply: 'Atheian. He was Donli Sairn, your master.'

'In that event, the possibility of tracking the desired local inhabitant may exist. The odds will now be computed. In the interim, do you wish to know the basis of the possibility?'

'Y-yes.'

'Native Atheian biochemistry developed in a manner quite parallel to Earth's,' said the voice, 'and the early colonists had no difficulty in introducing terrestrial species. Thus they enjoyed a friendly environment, where population soon grew sufficiently large to obviate the danger of racial change through mutation and/or genetic drift. In addition, no selection pressure tended to force change. Hence the modern Atheian human is little different from his ancestors of Earth, on which account his physiology and biochemistry are known in detail.

'This has been essentially the case on most colonized planets for which records are available. Where different breeds of men have arisen, it has generally been because the original settlers were highly selected groups. Randomness, and evolutionary adaptation to new conditions, have seldom produced radical changes in biotype. For example the robustness on the average Krakener is a response to comparatively high gravity, his size aids him in resisting cold, his fair complexion is helpful beneath a sun poor in ultraviolet. But his ancestors were people who already had the natural endowments for such a world. His deviations from their norm are not extreme. They do not preclude his living on more Earth-like planets or interbreeding with the inhabitants of these.

'Occasionally, however, larger variations have occurred. They appear to be due to a small original population or to unterrestroid conditions or both. The population may have been small because the planet could not support more, or have become small as the result of hostile action when the Empire fell. In the former case, genetic accidents had a chance to be significant; in the latter radiation produced a high rate of mutant births among survivors. The variations are less apt to be in gross anatomy than in subtle endocrine and enzymatic qualities, which affect the physiology and psychology. Well-known cases include the reaction of the Gwydiona to nicotine and certain indoles, and the requirement of the Ifrians for trace amounts of lead. Sometimes the inhabitants of two planets are actually intersterile because of their differences.

'While this world has hitherto received the sketchiest of examinations –' Evalyth was yanked out of the reverie into which the lecture had led her – 'certain facts appear. Few terrestrial species have flourished; no doubt others were introduced originally, but died off after the technology to maintain them was lost. Man has thus been forced to depend on autochthonous life for the major part of his food. This life is deficient in various elements of human nutrition. For example, the only Vitamin C appears to be on immigrant plants; Sairn observed that the people consume large amounts of grass and leaves from those species, and that fluoroscopic pictures indicate this practice had measurable modified the digestive tract. No one would supply skin, blood, sputum, or similar samples, not even from corpses.' *Afraid of magic*, Evalyth thought drearily, *yes, they're back to that too.* 'But intensive analysis of the usual meat animals shows these to be under-supplied with three essential amino-acids, and human adaptation to this must have involved considerable change on the cellular and sub-cellular levels. The probable type and extent of such change are computable.

'The calculations are now complete.' Evalyth gripped the arms of her chair and could not breathe. 'While the answer is subject to error for lack of precise data, it indicates a fair probability of success. In effect, Atheian flesh is alien here. It can be metabolized, but the body of the local consumer will excrete certain compounds and these will impart a characteristic odour to skin and breath as well as to urine and faeces. The chance is good that it will be detectable by neo-Freeholder technique at distances of several kilometres, after sixty or seventy hours. But since the molecules in question are steadily being degraded and dissipated, speed of action is recommended.'

I am going to find Donli's murderer. Darkness roared around Evalyth.

'Shall the organisms be ordered for you and given the appropriate search programme?' asked the voice. 'They can be on hand in an estimated three hours.'

'Yes,' she stammered. 'Oh, please – Have you any other . . . other . . . advice?'

'The man ought not to be killed out of hand, but brought here for examination: if for no other reason, then in order that the scientific ends of the expedition may be served.'

That's a machine talking, Evalyth cried. *It's designed to help research. Nothing more. But it was his.* And its answer was so altogether Donli that she could no longer hold back her tears.

The single big moon rose nearly full, shortly after sundown. It drowned most stars; the jungle beneath was cobbled with silver and dappled with black; the snowcone of Mount Burus floated unreal at the unseen edge of the world. Wind slid around Evalyth where she crouched on her gravsled; it was full of wet acrid odours, and felt cold though it was not, and chuckled at her back. Somewhere something screeched, every few minutes, and something else cawed reply.

She scowled at her position indicators aglow on the control panel. Curses and chaos, Moru had to be in this area! He couldn't have escaped from the valley on foot in the time available, and her search pattern had practically covered it. If she ran out of bugs before she found him, must she assume he was dead? They ought to be able to find his body regardless, ought they not? Unless it was buried deep – Here. She brought the sled to hover, took the next phial off the rack, and stood up to open it.

The bugs came out many and tiny, like smoke in the moonlight. Their cloud whirled, began to break apart. Evalyth felt a nausea. Another failure?

No! Wait! Were not those motes dancing back together, into a streak barely visible under the moon, and vanishing downward? Heart thuttering, she turned to the indicator. Its neurodetector antenna was not aimlessly wobbling but pointed straight west-north-west, declination thirty-two degrees below horizontal. Only a concentration of the bugs could make it behave like that. And only the particular mixture of molecules to which the bugs had been presensitized, in several parts per million or better, would make them converge on the source.

'Ya-a-a-ah!' She couldn't help the one hawk-yell. But thereafter she bit her lips shut – blood trickled unnoticed down her chin – and drove the sled in silence.

The distance was a mere few kilometres. She came to a halt above an opening in the forest. Pools of scummy water gleamed in its rank growth. The trees made a solid-seeming wall around. Evalyth clapped her night goggles down off her helmet and over her eyes. A lean-to became visible. It was hastily woven from vines and withes, huddled against a pair of the largest trees to let their branches hide it from the sky. The bugs were entering.

Evalyth lowered her sled to a metre off the ground and got to her feet again. A stun pistol slid from its sheath into her right hand. Her left rested on the blaster.

Moru's two sons groped from the shelter. The bugs whirled around them, a mist that blurred their outlines. *Of course,* Evalyth realized, nonetheless shocked into a higher hatred, *I should have known, they did the actual devouring.* More than ever did they resemble gnomes – skinny limbs, big heads, the pot bellies of under-nourishment. Krakener boys of their age would have twice their bulk and be noticeably on the way to becoming men. These nude bodies belonged to children, except that they had the grotesqueness of eld.

The parents followed them, ignored by the entranced bugs. The mother wailed. Evalyth identified a few words, 'What is the matter, what are those things – oh, help –' but her gaze was locked upon Moru.

Limping out of the hutch, stooped to clear its entrance, he made her think of some huge beetle crawling from an offal heap. But she would know that bushy head though her brain were coming apart. He carried a stone blade, surely the one that hacked up Donli. *I will take it away from him, and the hand with it,* Evalyth wept. *I will keep him alive while I dismantle him with these my own hands, and in between times he can watch me flay those repulsive spawn of his.*

The wife's scream broke through. She had seen the metal thing, and the giant that stood on its platform, with skull and eyes shimmering beneath the moon.

'I have come for you who killed my man,' Evalyth said.

The mother screamed anew and cast herself before the boys. The father tried to run around in front of her, but his lame foot twisted under him and he fell into a pool. As he struggled out of its muck, Evalyth shot the woman. No sound was heard; she folded and lay moveless. 'Run!' Moru shouted. He tried to charge the sled. Evalyth twisted a control stick. Her vehicle whipped in a circle, heading off the boys. She shot them from above, where Moru couldn't quite reach her.

He knelt beside the nearest, took the body in his arms and looked upward. The moonlight poured relentlessly across him. 'What can you now do to me?' he called.

She stunned him too, landed, got off and quickly hogtied the four of them. Loading them aboard, she found them lighter than she had expected.

Sweat had sprung forth upon her, until her coverall stuck dripping to her skin. She began to shake, as if with fever. Her ears buzzed. 'I would have destroyed you,' she said. Her voice sounded remote and unfamiliar. A still more distant part wondered why she bothered speaking to the unconscious, in her own tongue at that. 'I wish you hadn't acted the way you did. That made me remember what the computer said, about Donli's friends needing you for study.

'You're too good a chance, I suppose. After your doings, we have the right under allied rules to make prisoners of you, and none of his friends are likely to get maudlin about your feelings.

'Oh, they won't be inhumane. A few cell samples, a lot of tests, anaesthesia where necessary, nothing harmful, nothing but a clinical examination as thorough as facilities allow. No doubt you'll be better fed than at any time before, and no doubt the medics will find some pathologies they can cure for you. In the end, Moru, they'll release your wife and children.'

She stared into his horrible face. 'I am pleased,' she said 'that to you, who won't comprehend what is going on, it will be a bad experience. And when they are finished, Moru, I will insist on having you, at least back. They can't deny me that. Why, your tribe itself has, in effect cast you out. Right? My colleagues won't let me do more than kill you, I'm afraid, but on this I will insist.'

She gunned the engine and started towards Lokon, as fast as possible, to arrive while she felt able to be satisfied with that much.

And the days without him and the days without him.

The nights were welcome. If she had not worked herself quite to exhaustion, she could take a pill. He rarely returned in her dreams. But she had to get through each day, and would not drown him in drugs.

Luckily, there was a good deal of work involved in preparing to depart, when the expedition was short-handed and on short notice. Gear must be dismantled, packed, ferried to the ship, and stowed. *New Dawn* herself must be readied, numerous systems recommissioned and tested. Her militechnic training qualified Evalyth to double as mechanic, boat jockey, or loading gang boss. In addition, she kept up the routines of defence in the compound.

Captain Jonafer objected mildly to this. 'Why bother, Lieutenant? The locals are scared blue of us. They've heard what you did – and this coming and going through the sky, robots and heavy machinery in action, floodlights after dark – I'm having trouble persuading them not to abandon their town!'

'Let them,' she snapped. 'Who cares?'

'We did not come here to ruin them, Lieutenant.'

'No, In my judgement, though, Captain, they'll be glad to ruin us if we present the least opportunity. Imagine what special virtues *your* body must have.'

Jonafer sighed and gave in. But when she refused to receive Rogar the next time she was planetside, he ordered her to do so and be civil.

The *Klev* entered the biolab section – she would not have him in her living quarters – with a gift held in both hands, a sword of Imperial metal. She shrugged; no doubt a museum would be pleased to get the thing. 'Lay it on the floor,' she told him.

Because she occupied the single chair, he stood. He looked little and old in his robe. 'I came,' he whispered, 'to say how we of Lokon rejoice that the heaven-borne has won her revenge.'

'Is winning it,' she corrected.

He could not meet her eyes. She stared moodily at his faded hair. 'Since the heaven-borne could . . . easily . . . find those she wished . . . she knows the truth in the hearts of us of Lokon, that we never intended harm to her folk.'

That didn't seem to call for an answer.

His fingers twisted together. 'Then why do you forsake us?' he went on. 'When you first came, when we had come to know you and you spoke our speech, you said you would stay for many moons, and after you would come others to teach and trade. Our hearts rejoiced. It was not alone the goods you might someday let us buy, nor that your wisemen talked of ways to end hunger, sickness, danger, and sorrow. No, our jubilation and thankfulness were most for the wonders you opened. Suddenly the world was made great, that had been so narrow. And now you are going away. I have asked when I dared, and those of your men who will speak to me say none will return. How have we offended you, and how may it be made right, heaven-borne?'

81

'You can stop treating your fellow men like animals,' Evalyth got past her teeth.

'I have gathered . . . somewhat . . . that you from the stars say it is wrong what happened in the Sacred Place. But we only do it once in a lifetime, heaven-borne, and because we must.'

'You have no need.'

Rogar went on his hands and knees before her. 'Perhaps the heaven-borne are thus,' he pleaded, 'but we are merely men. If our sons do not get the manhood, they will never beget children of their own, and the last of us will die alone in a world of death, with none to crack his skull and let the soul out –' He dared glance up at her. What he saw made him whimper and crawl backwards into the sun-glare.

Later Chena Darnard sought Evalyth. They had a drink and talked around the subject for a while, until the anthropologist plunged in: 'You were pretty hard on the sachem, weren't you?'

'How'd you – Oh.' The Krakener remembered that the interview had been taped, as was done whenever possible for later study. 'What was I supposed to do, kiss his man-eating mouth?'

'No.' Chena winced. 'I suppose not.'

'Your signature heads the list, on the official recommendation that we quit this planet.'

'Yes. But – Now I don't know. I was repelled. I am. However – I've been observing the medical team working on those prisoners of yours. Have you?'

'No.'

'You should. The way they cringe and shriek, and reach to each other when they're strapped down in the lab, and cling together afterwards in their cell.'

'They aren't suffering pain or mutilation, are they?'

'Of course not. But can they believe it when their captors say they won't? They can't be tranquillized while under study you know, if the results are to be valid. Their fear of the absolutely unknown – Well, Evalyth, I had to stop observing. I couldn't take any more.' Chena gave the other a long stare. 'You might, though.'

Evalyth shook her head. 'I don't gloat. I'll shoot the murderer because my family honour demands it. The rest can go free, even the boys, even in spite of what they ate.' She poured herself a stiff draught and tossed it off in a gulp. The liquor burned on the way down.

'I wish you wouldn't,' Chena said. 'Donli wouldn't have liked it. He had a proverb that he claimed was very Ancient – he was from my city, don't forget, and I have known ... I did know him longer than you, dear – I heard him say, twice or thrice. *Do I not destroy my enemies if I make them my friends?*'

'Think of a venomous insect,' Evelyth replied. 'You don't make friends with it. You put it under your heel.'

'But a man does what he does because of what he is, what his society had made him.' Chena's voice grew urgent; she leaned forward to grip Evalyth's hand, which did not respond. 'What is one man, one lifetime, against all who live around him and all who have gone before? Cannibalism wouldn't be found everywhere over this island, in every one of these otherwise altogether different groupings, if it weren't the most deeply rooted cultural imperative this race has got.'

Evalyth grinned around a rising anger. 'And what kind of race are they to acquire it? And how about according me the privilege of operating my own cultural imperatives? I'm bound home, to raise Donli's child away from your gutless civilization. He will not grow up disgraced because his mother was too weak to exact justice for his father. Now if you'll excuse me, I have to get up early and take another boatload to the ship and get it inboard.'

That task required a while. Evalyth came back towards sunset the next day. She felt a little more tired than usual, a little more peaceful. The raw edge of what had happened was healing over. The thought crossed her mind, abstract but not shocking, not disloyal: *I'm young. One year another man will come. I won't love you the less, darling*.

Dust scuffed under her boots. The compound was half stripped already, a corresponding number of personnel berthed in the ship. The evening reached quiet beneath a yellowing sky. Only a few of the expedition stirred among the machines and remaining cabins. Lokon lay as hushed as it had lately become. She welcomed the thud of her footfalls on the steps into Jonafer's office.

He sat waiting for her, big and unmoving behind his desk. 'Assignment completed without incident,' she reported.

'Sit down,' he said.

She obeyed. The silence grew. At last he said, out of a stiff face: 'The clinical team has finished with the prisoners.'

Somehow it was a shock. Evalyth groped for words: 'Isn't that too soon? I mean, well, we don't have a lot of equipment, and just a couple of men who can use the advanced stuff, and then without Donli for an expert on Earth biology – Wouldn't a good

83

study go down to the chromosomal level if not further – something that the physical anthropologists could use – wouldn't it take longer?'

'That's correct,' Jonafer said. 'Nothing of major importance was found. Perhaps something would have been, if Uden's team had any inkling of what to look for. Given that, they could have made hypotheses, and tested them in a whole-organism context, and come to some understandings of their subjects as functioning beings. You're right, Donli Sairn had the kind of professional intuition that might have guided them. Lacking that, and with no particular clues, and no co-operation from those ignorant, terrified savages, they had to grope and probe almost at random. They did establish a few digestive peculiarities – nothing that couldn't have been predicted on the basis of ambient ecology.'

'Then why have they stopped? We won't be leaving for another week at the earliest.'

'They did so on my orders, after Uden had shown me what was going on and said he'd quit regardless of what I wanted.'

'What –? Oh.' Scorn lifted Evalyth's head. 'You mean the psychological torture.'

'Yes, I saw that scrawny woman secured to a table. Her head her body were covered with leads to the meters that clustered around her and clicked and hummed and flickered. She didn't see me; her eyes were blind with fear. I suppose she imagined her soul was being pumped out. Or maybe the process was worse for being something she couldn't put a name to, I saw her kids in a cell, holding hands. Nothing else left for them to hold on to, in their total universe. They're just at puberty; what'll this do to their psychosexual development? I saw their father lying drugged beside them, after he'd tried to batter his way straight through the wall. Uden and his helpers told me how they'd tried to make friends and failed. Because naturally the prisoners know they're in the power of those who hate them with a hate that goes beyond the grave.'

Jonafer paused. 'There are decent limits to everything, Lieutenant,' he ended, 'including science and punishment. Especially when, after all, the chance of discovering anything else unusual is slight. I ordered the investigation terminated. The boys and their mother will be flown to their home area and released tomorrow.'

'Why not today?' Evelyth asked, foreseeing his reply.

'I hoped,' Jonafer said, 'that you'd agree to let the man go with them.'

'No.'

'In the name of God –'

'Your God.' Evalyth looked away from him. 'I won't enjoy it, Captain. I'm beginning to wish I didn't have to. But it's not as if Donli'd been killed in an honest war or feud or – He was slaughtered like a pig. That's the evil in cannibalism; it makes a man nothing but another meat animal. I won't bring him back, but I will somehow even things, by making the cannibal nothing but a dangerous animal that needs shooting.'

'I see.' Jonafer too stared long out of the window. In the sunset light his face became a mask of brass. 'Well,' he said finally, coldly, 'under the Charter of the Alliance and the articles of this expedition, you leave me no choice. But we will not have any ghoulish ceremonies, and you will not deputize what you want done. The prisoner will be brought to your place privately after dark. You will dispose of him at once and assist in cremating the remains.'

Evalyth's palms grew wet. *I never killed a helpless man before!*

But he did, it answered. 'Understood Captain,' she said.

'Very good, Lieutenant. You may go clean up and join the mess for dinner if you wish. No announcements to anyone. The business will be scheduled for –' Jonafer glanced at his watch, set to local rotation – '2600 hours.'

Evalyth swallowed around a clump of dryness. 'Isn't that rather late?'

'On purpose,' he told her. 'I want the camp asleep.' His glance struck hers. 'And want you to have time to reconsider.'

'No!' She sprang erect and went for the door.

His voice pursued her: 'Donli would have asked you for that.'

Night came in and filled the room. Evalyth didn't rise to turn on the light. It was as if this chair, which had been Donli's favourite, wouldn't let her go.

Finally she remembered the psychodrugs. She had a few tablets left. One of them would make the execution easy to perform. No doubt Jonafer would direct that Moru be tranquilized – now, at last – before they brought him here. So why should she not give herself calmness?

It wouldn't be right.

Why not?

I don't know. I don't understand anything any longer.

85

Who does? Moru alone. He knows why he murdered and butchered a man who trusted him. Evalyth found herself smiling wearily into the darkness. *He has a superstition for his sure guide. He's actually seen his children display the first signs of maturity. That ought to console him a little.*

Odd, that the glandular upheaval of adolescence should have commenced under frightful stress. One would have expected a delay instead. True the captives had been getting a balanced diet for a change and medicine had probably eliminated various chronic low-level infections. Nonetheless the fact was odd. Besides, normal children under normal conditions would not develop the outward signs beyond mistaking in this short a time. Donli would have puzzled over the matter. She could almost see him, frowning, rubbing his forehead, grinning one-sidedly with the pleasure of a problem.

'I'd like to have a go at this myself,' she heard him telling Uden over a beer and a smoke. 'Might turn up an angle.'

'How?' the medic would have replied. 'You're a general biologist. No reflection on you, but detailed human physiology is out of your line.'

'Um-m-m . . .yes and no. My main job is studying species of terrestrial origin and how they've adapted to new planets. By a remarkable coincidence, man is included among them.'

But Donli was gone, and no one else was competent to do his work – to be any part of him, but she fled from that thought and from the thought of what she must presently do. She held her mind tightly to the realization that none of Uden's team had tried to apply Donli's knowledge. As Jonafer remarked, a living Donli might well have suggested an idea, unorthodox and insightful, that would have led to the discovery of whatever was there to be discovered, if anything was. Uden and his assistants were routineers. They hadn't even thought to make Donli's computer ransack its data banks for possibly relevant information. Why should they when they saw their problems as strictly medical? And, to be sure they were not cruel. The anguish they were inflicting had made them avoid whatever might lead to ideas demanding further research. Donli would have approached the entire business differently from the outset.

Suddenly the gloom thickened. Evalyth fought for breath. Too hot and silent here; too long a wait; she must do something or her will would desert her and she would be unable to squeeze the trigger.

86

She stumbled to her feet and into the lab. The fluoro blinded her for a moment when she turned it on. She went to his computer and said: 'Activate!'

Nothing responded but the indicator light. The windows were totally black. Clouds outside shut off moon and stars.

'What –' The sound was a curious croak. But that brought a releasing call: *Take hold of yourself, you blubbering idiot, or you're not fit to mother the child you're carrying*. She could then ask questions. 'What explanations in terms of biology can be devised for the behaviour of the people on this planet?'

'Matters of that nature are presumably best explained in terms of psychology and cultural anthropology,' said the voice.

'M-m-maybe,' Evalyth said. 'And maybe not.' She marshalled a few thoughts and stood them firm amidst the others roiling in her skull. 'The inhabitants could be degenerate somehow, not really human.' *I want Moru to be.* 'Scan every fact recorded about them, including the detailed clinical observations made on four of them in the past several days. Compare with basic terrestrial data. Give me whatever hypotheses looks reasonable.' She hesitated. 'Correction. I mean possible hypotheses – anything that doesn't flatly contradict established facts. We've used up the reasonable ideas already.'

The machine hummed. Evalyth closed her eyes and clung to the edge of the desk. *Donli, please help me.*

At the other end of forever, the voice came to her:

'The sole behavioural element which appears to be not easily explicable by postulates concerning environment and accidental historical developments, is the cannibalistic puberty rite. According to the anthropological computer, this might well have originated as a form of human sacrifice. But that computer notes certain illogicalities in the idea, as follows.

'On Old Earth, sacrificial religion was normally associated with agricultural societies, which were more vitally dependent on continued fertility and good weather than hunters. Even for them, the offering of humans proved disadvantageous in the long run, as the Aztec example most clearly demonstrates. Lokon has rationalized the practice to a degree, making it part of the slavery system and thus minimizing its impact on the generality. But for the lowlanders it is a powerful evil, a source of perpetual danger, a diversion of effort and resources that are badly needed for survival. It is not plausible that the custom, if ever imitated from Lokon, should persist among every one of those tribes. Nevertheless it does. Therefore it must have some value and the problem is to find what.

'The method of obtaining victims varies widely, but the requirements always appear to be the same. According to the Lokonese, one adult male body is necessary and sufficient for the maturation of four boys. The killer of Donli Sairn was unable to carry the entire corpse. What he did take of it is suggestive.

'Hence a dipteroid phenomenon may have appeared in man on this planet. Such a thing is unknown among higher animals elsewhere, but it is conceivable. A modification of the Y chromosome would produce it. The test for that modification, and thus the test of the hypothesis, is easily made.'

The voice stopped. Evalyth heard the blood slugging in her veins. 'What are you talking about?'

'The phenomenon is found among lower animals on lower worlds,' the computer told her. 'It is uncommon and so is not widely known. The name derives from the Diptera, a type of dung fly on Old Earth.'

Lightning flickered: 'Dung fly – good, yes!'

The machine went on to explain.

Jonafer came alone with Moru. The savage's hands were tied behind his back, and the spaceman loomed enormous over him. Despite that and the bruises he had inflicted on himself, he hobbled along steadily. The clouds were breaking and the moon shone ice-white. Where Evalyth waited, outside her door, she saw the compound reach bare to the saw-topped stockade and a crane stand above like a gibbet. The air was growing cold – the planet spinning towards an autumn – and a small wind had arisen to whimper behind the dust devils that stirred across the earth. Jonafer's footfalls rang loud.

He noticed her and stopped. Moru did likewise. 'What did they learn?' she asked.

The captain nodded. 'Uden got right to work when you called,' he said. 'The test is more complicated than your computer suggested – but then, it's for Donli's kind of skill, not Uden's. He'd never have thought of it unassisted. Yes, the notion is true.'

'How?'

Moru stood waiting while the language he did not understand went to and fro around him.

'I'm no medic.' Jonafer kept his tone altogether colourless. 'But from what Uden told me, the chromosome defect means that the male gonads here can't mature spontaneously. They need an extra supply of hormones – he mentioned testosterone and androsterone, I forget what else – to start off the series of changes which bring on puberty. Lacking that, you'll get eunuchism. Uden thinks the surviving population was tiny after the colony was bombed out, and so poor that it resorted to cannibalism for bare survival, the first generation or two. Under those circumstances, a mutation that would otherwise have eliminated itself got established and spread to every descendant.'

Evalyth nodded. 'I see.'

'You understand what this means, I suppose,' Jonafer said. There'll be no problem to ending this practice. We'll simply tell them we have a new and better Holy Food, and prove it with a few pills. Terrestrial-type meat animals can be reintroduced later and supply what's necessary. In the end, no doubt our geneticists can repair that faulty Y chromosome.'

He could not stay contained any longer. His mouth opened, a gash across his half-seen face, and he rasped: 'I should praise you for saving a whole people. I can't. Get your business over with, will you?'

Evalyth trod forward to stand before Moru. He shivered but met her eyes. Astonished she said: 'You haven't drugged him.'

'No,' Jonager said. 'I wouldn't help you.' He spat.

'Well, I'm glad.' She addressed Moru in his own language: 'You killed my man. Is it right that I should kill you?'

'It is right,' he answered almost as levelly as she. 'I thank you that my woman and my sons are to go free.' He was quiet for a second or two. 'I have heard that your folk can preserve food for years without it rotting. I would be glad if you kept my body to give your sons.'

'Mine will not need it,' Evalyth said. 'Nor will the sons of your sons.'

Anxiety tinged his words: 'Do you know why I slew your man? He was kind to me, and like a god. But I am lame. I saw no other way to get what my sons must have; and they must have it soon, or it would be too late and they could never become men.'

'He taught me,' Evalyth said, 'how much it is to be a man.'

She turned to Jonafer, who stood tense and puzzled. 'I had my revenge,' she said in Donli's tongue.

'What?' His question was a reflexive pose.

'After I learned about the dipteroid phenomenon,' she said. 'All that was necessary was for me to keep silent. Moru, his children,

89

his entire race would go on being prey for centuries, maybe forever. I sat for half an hour, I think, having my revenge.'

'And then?' Jonafer asked.

'I was satisfied, and could start thinking about justice,' Evalyth said.

She drew a knife. Moru straightened his back. She stepped behind him and cut his bonds. 'Go home,' she said. 'Remember him.'

James Blish

A HERO'S LIFE

1

Listening automatically for the first sound of possible interruption, Simon de Kuyl emptied his little poisons into the catch basin in his room and ironically watched the wisps of wine-coloured smoke rise from the corroded maw of the drain. He was sorry to see them go; they were old though venemous friends.

He knew without vanity – it was too late for that – that High Earth had no more distinguished a traitor than he. But after only four clockless days on Boadicea, he had already found it advisable to change his name, his methods and his residence. It was a humiliating beginning.

The almost worn-away legend on the basin read: *Julius Boadicea*. Things made on this planet were usually labelled that generally, as though any place in the world were like every other, but this both was and was not true. The present city, Druidsfall, was the usual low jumble of decayed masonry, slightly less ancient slums and blank-faced offices, but the fact that it was also the centre of the treason industry – hence wholly convenient for Simon – gave it character. The traitors had an architectural style of their own, characterized by structures put together mostly of fragmented statues and petrified bodies fitted like puzzle-pieces or maps. Traitors on Boadicea had belonged to an honoured social class for four hundred years, and their edifices made it known.

Luckily custom allowed Simon to stay clear of these buildings after the first formalities and seek out his own bed and breakfast. In the old friendly inns of Druidsfall, the anonymous thumps of the transients – in death, love or trade – are said to make the lodgers start in their beds with their resident guilts. Of course all inns are like that; but nevertheless, that is why the traitors like to quarter there, rather than in the Traitors' Halls: it guarantees them privacy, and at the same time helps them to feel alive. There is undoubtedly something inhibiting about trying to deal within walls pieced together of broken stone corpses.

Here in The Skopolamander, Simon awaited his first contact. This – now that he had dumped his poisons – would fall at the end of his immunity period. Quarantine was perhaps a more appropriate term . . .

No, the immunity was real, however limited, for as a traitor to High Earth he had special status. High Earth, the Boadiceans thought, was not necessarily Old Earth – but not necessarily not, either. For twelve days Simon would not be killed out of sheer conservatism, at least, though nobody would attempt to deal with him, either.

He had three of those days still to run – a dull prospect, since he had already completed every possible preliminary, and spiced only by the fact that he had yet to figure out how long a day might be. Boadicea's sun was a ninety-minute microvariable, twinned at a distance of a light-year with a bluewhite, Rigel-like star which stood – or had stood throughout historical times – in high Southern latitudes. This gave Druidsfall only four consecutive hours of quasi-darkness at a time, and even during this period the sky was indigo rather than black at its deepest, and more often than not flaring with aurorae. There was one lighting the window now, looking like a curtain of orange and hazy blue fire licking upward along a bone trellis.

Everything in the city, as everywhere upon Boadicea, bespoke the crucial importance of fugitive light, and the fade-out-fade-in weather that went with it, all very strange after the desert glare of High Earth. The day of Simon's arrival had dawned in mist, which cold gales had torn away into slowly pulsating sunlight; then had come clouds and rain which had turned to snow and then to sleet – more weather in a day than the minarets of Novoe Jiddah, Simon's registered home town, saw in a six-month. The fluctuating light and wetness was reflected in Druidsfall most startlingly by its gardens, which sprang up when one's back was turned and did not need to be so much weeded as actually fought. They were constantly in motion to the ninety-minute solar cycle, battering their elaborate heads against back walls which were everywhere crumbling after centuries of such soft, implacable impacts. Half the buildings in Druidsfall glistened with their leaves, which were scaled with so much soft gold that they stuck to anything they were blown against – the wealth of Boadicea was based anciently in the vast amounts of uranium and other power-metals in its soil, from which the plants extracted the inevitable associated gold as radiation shielding for their spuriously tender genes. Everyone one saw in the streets of Druidsfall, or any other such city, was a mutation of some sort – if he was not an out-worlder – but after a day in the winds they were all half yellow, for the gold scales smeared off the flying leaves like butter; everyone was painted with meaningless riches, the very bed-sheets glittered ineradicably with flakes of it, and brunettes – especially among the elaborate hair-styles of the men – were at a premium.

Simon poured water from an amphora into the basin, which promptly hissed like a dragon just out of the egg and blurted a mushroom of cold blue steam which made him cough. Careful! he thought; acid after water, never water after acid – I am for-getting the most elementary lessons. I should have used wine. Time for a drink, in Gro's name!

He caught up his cloak and went out, not bothering to lock the door. He had nothing worth stealing but his honour which was in his right hip pocket. Oh, and of course, High Earth – that was in his left. Besides, Boadicea was rich: one could hardly turn around without knocking over some heap of treasures, artifacts of a millenium which nobody had sorted for a century or even wanted to be bothered to sort. Nobody would think to steal from a poor traitor any object smaller than a king, or preferably a planet.

In the tavern below, Simon was joined at once by a play-woman. 'Are you buying tonight excellence?'

'Why not?' And in fact he was glad to see her. She was blonde and ample, a relief from the sketchy women of the Respectables whom fashion made look as though they suffered from some nervous disease that robbed them of appetite. Besides she would exempt him from the normal sort of Boadicean polite conversation which consisted chiefly of elaborately involuted jokes at which it was considered gauche to laugh. The whole style of Boadicean conversation for that matter was intended to be ignored; gambits were a high art but end-games were a lost one. Simon sighed and signalled for beakers.

'You wear the traitors' clasp,' she said, sitting across from him, 'but not much tree-gold. Have you come to sell us High Earth?'

Simon did not even blink; he knew the query to be a standard opening with any outworlder of his profession.

'Perhaps. But I'm not on business at the moment.'

'Of course not,' the girl said gravely, her fingers playing continuously with a sort of rosary tasselled with two silver phalluses. 'Yet I hope you prosper. My half-brother is a traitor, but he can find only small secrets to sell – how to make bombs, and the like. It's a thin life; I prefer mine.'

'Perhaps he should swear by another country.'

'Oh, his country is well worth selling, but his custom is poor. Neither buyer nor seller trusts him very far – a matter of style, I suppose. He'll probably wind up betraying some colony for a thousand beans and a fish-ball.'

'You dislike the man – or is it the trade?' Simon said. 'It seems not unlike your own, after all: one sells something one never really owned, and yet one still has it when the transaction is over, as long as both parties keep silent.'

'You dislike women,' the girl said, tranquilly, as a simple observation, not a challenge. 'But all things are loans – not just chastity and trust. Why be miserly. To "possess" wealth is as illusory as to "possess" honour or a woman, and much less gratifying. Spending is better than saving.'

'But there are rank orders in all things, too.' Simon said, lighting a kief stick. He was intrigued in spite of himself. Hedonism was the commonest of philosophies in the civilized galaxy, but it was piquant to hear a playwoman trotting out its mouldy clichés with such fierce solemnity. 'Otherwise we should never know the good from the bad, or care.'

'Do you like boys?'

'No, that's not one of my tastes. Ah: you will say that I don't condemn boy-lovers, and that values are in the end only preferences? I think not. In morals, empathy enters in, eventually.'

'So: you wouldn't corrupt children, and torture revolts you. But Gro made you that way. Some men are not so handicapped. I meet them now and then.' The hand holding the looped beads made a small, unconcious gesture of revulsion.

'I think they are the handicapped, not I – most planets hang their moral imbeciles, sooner or later. But what about treason? You didn't answer that question.'

'My throat was dry . . . thank you. Treason, well – it's an art,

94

hence again a domain of taste or preference. Style is everything; that's why my half-brother is so inept. If tastes changed he might prosper, as I might had I been born with blue hair.'

'You could dye it.'

'What, like the Respectables?' She laughed, briefly but un-affectedly. 'I am what I am; disguises don't become me. Skills, yes – those are another matter. I'll show you, when you like. But no masks.'

Skills can betray you too, Simon thought, remembering that moment at the Traitors' Guild when his proud sash of poison shells had lost him in an instant every inch of altitude over the local professionals that he had hoped to trade on. But he only said again, 'Why not?' It would be as good a way as any to while away the time; and once his immunity had expired he could never again trust a playwoman on Boadicea.

She proved, indeed, very skilful, and the time passed . . . but the irregular days – the clock in the tavern was on a different time from the one in his room, and neither even faintly agreed with his High Earth based chronometer and metabolism – betrayed him. He awoke one morning/noon/night to find the girl turning slowly black beside him, in the last embrace of a fungal toxin he would have reserved for the Emperor of Canes Venatici or the worst criminal in human history.

War had been declared. He had been notified that if he still wanted to sell High Earth, he would first have to show his skill at staying alive against the whole cold malice of all the Traitors of Boadicea.

II

He holed up quickly and drastically, beginning with a shot of transduction serum – an almost insanely dangerous expedient, for the stuff not only altered his appearance but his very heredity, leaving his head humming with false memories and traces of character, derived from the unknown donors of the serum, which conflicted not only with his purposes but even with his tastes and motives. Under interrogation he would break down into a bab-bling crowd of random voices, as bafflingly scrambled as his blood types and his retina – and finger prints, and to the eyes his gross physical appearance would be a vague characterless blur of many rôles – some of them derived from the D.N.A. of persons who had died a hundred years ago and at least that many parsecs away in space – but unless he got the anti-serum within fifteen days, he would first forget his mission, then his skills, and at last his very identity. Nevertheless, he judged that the risk had to be taken; for effete though the local traitors seemed to be, they were obviously quite capable of penetrating any lesser cover.

The next problem was how to complete the mission itself – it would not be enough just to stay alive. After all, he was still no ordinary traitor, nor even the usual kind of double agent; his task was to buy Boadicea while seeming to sell High Earth, but beyond that, there was a grander treason in the making for which the combined guilds of both planets might only barely be sufficient – the toppling of the Green Exarch, under whose subtle non-human yoke half of humanity's worlds had not even the latter-day good sense to groan. For such a project, the wealth of Boadicea was a pre-requisite, for the Green Exarch drew tithes from six fallen empires older than man – the wealth of Boadicea, and its reputation as the first colony to break with Old Earth, back in the first days of the Imaginary Drive.

And therein lay the difficulty, for Boadicea, beyond all other colony worlds, had fallen into a kind of autumn cannibalism. In defiance of that saying of Ezra-Tse, the edge was attempting to eat the centre. It was this worship of independence or rather, autonomy, which had not only made treason respectable, but had come nigh on to ennobling it . . . and was now imperceptibly emasculating it, like the statues one saw everywhere in Druidsfall which had been defaced and sexually mutilated by the grey disease of time and the weather.

Today, though all the Boadiceans proper were colonials in ancestry, they were snobs about their planet's pre-human history as though they had themselves not nearly exterminated the aborigines but were their inheritors. The few shambling Chariot-eers who still lived stumbled through the streets of Druidsfall loaded with ritual honours, carefully shorn of real power but ostentatiously deferred to on the slightest occasion which might be noticed by anyone from High Earth. In the meantime, the Boadiceans sold each other out with delicate enthusiasm, but against High Earth – which was not necessarily Old Earth, but not necessarily was not, either – all gates were formally locked.

Formally only, Simon and High Earth were sure; for the habit of treason, like lechery, tends to grow with what it feeds on, and to lose discrimination in the process. Boadicea, like all forbidden fruits, should be ripe for the plucking, for the man with the proper key to its neglected garden.

The key that Simon had brought with him was now lost; he would have to forge another, with whatever crude tools could be made to fall to hand. The only one accessible to Simon at the moment was the dead playwoman's despised half-brother.

His name, Simon had found easily enough, was currently Da-Ud tam Altair, and he was Court Traitor to a small religious principate on the Gulf of the Rood, on the edge of The InContinent, half the world away from Druidsfall. Since one of his duties was that of singing the Rood-Prince to sleep to the accompaniment of a sareh, a sort of gleemans harp (actually a Charioteer instrument ill-adapted to human |fingers, and which Da-Ud played worse than most of those who affected it), Simon reached him readily in the guise of a ballad-merchant, selling him twelve-and-a-tilly of ancient High Earth songs Simon had made up while in transit to the principate; it was as easy as giving Turkish Delight to a baby.

After the last mangled chord died, Simon told Da-Ud quietly:

'By the way . . . well sung, excellence . . . did you know that the Guild has murdered your half-sister?'

Da-Ud dropped the fake harp with a noise like a spring-toy coming unwound.

'Jillith? But she was only a playwoman! Why, in Gro's name –'

Then Da-Ud caught himself and stared at Simon with sudden, belated suspicion. Simon looked back, waiting.

'Who told you that? Damn you – are you a Torturer? I haven't – I've done nothing to merit –'

'I'm not a Torturer, and nobody told me,' Simon said. 'She died in my bed, as a warning to me.'

He removed his Clasp from the shoulder of his cloak and clicked it. The little machine flowered briefly into a dazzling actinic glare, and then closed again. While Da-Ud was still covering his streaming eyes, Simon said softly:

'I am the Traitor-in-Chief of High Earth.'

It was not the flash of the badge that was dazzling Da-Ud now. He lowered his hands. His whole plump body was trembling with hate and eagerness.

'What – what do you want of me, excellence? I have nothing to sell but the Rood-Prince . . . and a poor stick he is. Surely you would not sell me High Earth; I am a poor stick myself.'

'I would sell you High Earth for twenty riyals.'

'You mock me!'

'No, Da-Ud. I came here to deal with the Guild, but they killed Jillith – and that as far as I'm concerned disqualified them from

97

being treated with as civilized professionals, or as human beings at all. She was pleasant and intelligent and I was fond of her – and besides, while I'm perfectly willing to kill under some conditions, I don't hold with throwing away an innocent life for some footling dramatic gesture.'

'I wholly agree,' Da-Ud said. His indignation seemed to be at least half real. 'But what will you do? What *can* you do?'

'I have to fulfil my mission, any way short of my own death – if I die, nobody will be left to get it done. But I'd most dearly love to cheat, dismay, disgrace the Guild in the process, if it could possibly be managed. I'll need your help. If we live through it, I'll see to it that you'll turn a profit, too; money isn't my first goal here, or even my second now.'

'I'll tackle it,' Da-Ud said at once, though he was obviously apprehensive, as was only sensible. 'What precisely do you propose?'

'First of all, I'll supply you with papers indicating that I've sold you a part – not all – of the major thing I have to sell, which gives the man who holds it a lever in the State Ministry of High Earth. It shows that High Earth has been conspiring against several major powers, all human, for purposes of gaining altitude with the Green Exarch. They won't tell you precisely which worlds, but there will be sufficient information there so that the Exarchy would pay a heavy purse for them – and high Earth an even heavier one to get them back.

'It will be your understanding that the missing information is also for sale, but you haven't got the price.'

'Suppose the Guild doesn't believe that?'

'They'll never believe – excuse me, I must be blunt – that you could have afforded the whole thing; they'll know I sold you *this* much of it only because I have a grudge, and you can tell them so – though I wouldn't expose the nature of the grudge if I were you. Were you unknown to them they might assume that you were me in disguise, but luckily they know you, and, ah, probably tend rather to underestimate you.'

'Kindly put,' Da-Ud said with a grin. 'But that won't prevent them from assuming that I know your whereabouts, or have some way of reaching you. They'll interrogate for that, and of course I'll tell them. I know them, too; it would be impossible not to tell, and I prefer to save myself needless pain.'

'Of course – don't risk interrogation at all, tell them you want to sell *me* out, as well as the secret. That will make sense to them, and I think they must have rules against interrogating a member who offers to sell; most Traitors' Guilds do.'

'True, but they'll observe them only so long as they believe me; that's standard too.'

Simon shrugged, 'Be convincing then,' he said. 'I have already said that this project will be dangerous; presumably you didn't become a traitor for sweet safety's sole sake.'

'No, but not for suicide's either. But I'll abide the course. Where are the documents?'

'Give me access to your Prince's toposcope-scriber and I'll produce them. But first – twenty riyals, please.'

'Minus two riyals for the use of the Prince's property. Bribes, you know.'

'Your sister was wrong, you do have style, in a myopic sort of way. All right, eighteen riyals – and then let's get on to real business. My time is not my own – not by a century.'

'But how do I reach you thereafter?'

'That information,' Simon said blandly, 'will cost you those other two riyals, and cheap at the price.'

III

The Rood-Prince's brain-dictation laboratory was very far from being up to Guild standards, let alone High Earth's, but Simon was satisfied that the documents he generated there would pass muster. They were utterly authentic, and every experienced traitor had a feeling for that quality, regardless of such technical deficiencies as blurry image registration and irrelevant emotional overtones.

That done, Simon began to consider how he would meet Da-Ud when the game had that much furthered itself. The arrangement he had made with the playwoman's half-brother was of course a blind, indeed a double blind, but it had to have the virtues of its imperfections or nothing would be accomplished. Yet Simon was now beginning to find it hard to think; the transduction serum was increasingly taking hold, and there were treasons taking place inside his skull which had nothing to do with Boadicea, the Green Exarch or High Earth. Worse: they seemed to have nothing to do with Simon de Kuyl, either, but instead muttered away about silly little provincial intrigues nothing could have brought him to care about – yet which made him feel irritated, angry, even ill, like a man in the throes of jealousy toward some predecessor and unable to reason them away. Knowing their source, he fought them studiously, but he knew they would get steadily worse, however resolute he was; they were coming out of his genes and his bloodstream, not his once finely honed, now dimming conciousness.

Under the circumstances, he was not going to be able to trust himself to see through very many highly elaborate schemes, so that it would be best to eliminate all but the most necessary. Hence it seemed better, after all, to meet Da-Ud in the Principate as arranged, and save the double dealing for more urgent occasions.

On the other hand, it would be foolish to hang around the Principate, waiting and risking some miscarriage – such as betrayal through a possible interrogation of Da-Ud – when there were things he might be accomplishing elsewhere. Besides, the unvarying foggy warmth and the fragmented garish religiousness of the Principate both annoyed him and exercised pulls of conflicting enthusiasms and loyalties on several of his mask personalities, who had apparently been as unstable even when whole as their bits and pieces had now made him. He was particularly out of sympathy with the motto graven on the lintel of the Rood-Prince's vaguely bird-shaped palace: JUSTICE IS LOVE. The sentiment, obviously descended from some colonial Islamic sect, was excellent doctrine for a culture given to treason, for it allowed the prosecution of almost any kind of betrayal on the grounds that Justice was being pursued; but Simon found it entirely too pat. Besides, he was suspicious of all abstractions which took the form 'A is B', in his opinion, neither justice nor mercy were very closely related to love, let alone being identical with it.

These bagatelles aside it seemed likely to Simon that something might be gained by returning for a while to Druidsfall and haunting the vicinity of the Guild Hall. At the worst, his address would then be unknown to Da-Ud, and his anonymity more complete in a larger city, the Guild less likely to identify him even were it to suspect him – as of course it would – of such boldness. At best, he might pick up some bit of useful information, particularly if Da-Ud's embassy were to create any unusual stir.

For a while he saw nothing unusual which was in itself fractionally reassuring: either the Guild was not alarmed by Da-Ud, or was not letting it show. On several days in succession, Simon saw the Boadicean Traitor-in-Chief enter and leave, sometimes with an entourage, more often with only a single slave: Valkol

'The Polite', a portly, jowly man in a black abah decorated only by the Clasp, with a kindly and humorous expression into which were set eyes like two bites of an iceberg. This was normal, although it gave Simon a small, ambiguous *frisson* which was all the more disturbing because he was unsure which of his *personae* he should assign it to: certainly not to his fundamental self, for although Valkol was here the predestined enemy, he was no more formidable that others Simon had defeated (while, it was true, being in his whole and right mind).

Then Simon recognized the 'slave', and ran.

There was no possibility of his identifying *who* the creature was; he was fortunate – in no way he could explain – to be able to penetrate just to *what* it was. The 'slave' was a vombis, or what in one of the oldest languages was called a Proteus, a creature which could imitate perfectly almost any life-form within its size range. Or nearly perfectly; for Simon, like one in perhaps five thousand of his colleagues, was sensitive to them, without ever being able to specify in what particular their imitations of humanity were deficient; other people, even those of the sex opposite to the one the vombis assumed, could find no flaw in them. In part because they do not revert when killed, no human had ever seen their 'real' form – if they had one – though of course there were legends aplenty. The talent might have made them ideal double agents, were it possible to trust them – but that was only an academic speculation since the vombis were wholly creatures of the Green Exarch.

Simon's first impulse, like that of any other human being, had been to kill this one instantly upon recognition, but that course had many obvious drawbacks. Besides, the presence of an agent of the Exarchy so close to the heart of this imbroglio was suggestive and might be put to some use. Of course the vombis might be in Druidsfall on some other business entirely, but Simon would be in no hurry to make so dangerous an assumption. No, it was altogether more likely that the Exarch, who could hardly have heard yet of Simon's arrival and disgrace, was simply aware in general of how crucial Boadicea would be to any scheme of High Earth's – he was above all an efficient tyrant – and had placed his creature here to keep an eye on things.

Yes, that situation might be used, if Simon could just keep his disquietingly percolating brains under control. Among his present advantages was the fact that his disguise was better than that of the vombis, a fact the creature was probably constitutionally incapable of suspecting. With a grim chuckle which he hoped he would not later regret, Simon flew back to the Gulf of the Rood.

Da-Ud met Simon in the Singing Gardens, a huge formal maze not much frequented of late even by lovers, because the Rood-Prince in the throes of some new religious crotchet had let it run wild, so that one had constantly to be fending off the ardour of the flowers. At best it made even simple conversation difficult, and it was rumoured that deep in the heart of the maze, the floral attentions were of a more sinister sort.

Da-Ud was exultant, indeed almost manic in his enthusiasm, which did not advance comprehension either; but Simon listened patiently.

'They bought it like lambs,' Da-Ud said, naming a sacrificial animal of High Earth so casually as to make one of Simon's *personae* shudder inside him. 'I had a little difficulty with the underlings, but not as much as I'd expected, and I got it all the way up to Valkol himself.'

'No sign of any outside interest?'

'No, nothing. I didn't let out any more than I had to until I reached His Politeness, and after that he put the blue seal on everything – wouldn't discuss anything but the weather while anyone else was around. Listen, Simon, I don't want to seem to be telling you your business, but I think I may know the Guild better than you do, and it seems to me that you're underplaying your hand. This thing is worth *money*.'

'I said it was.'

'Yes, but I don't think you've any conception how much. Old Valkol took my asking price without a murmur, in fact so fast that I'd wished I'd asked for twice as much. Just to show you I'm convinced of all this, I'm going to give it all to you.'

'Don't want it,' Simon said. 'Money is of no use to me unless I can complete the mission. All I need now is operating expenses, and I've got enough for that.'

This clearly had been what Da-Ud had hoped he would say, but Simon suspected that had matters gone otherwise, the younger man might indeed have given over as much as half the money. His enthusiasm mounted.

'All right, but that doesn't change the fact that we could be letting a fortune slip here.'

'How much?'

'Oh, at least a couple of megariyals – and I mean *apiece*,' Da-

Ud said grandly. 'I can't imagine an opportunity like that comes around very often, even in the circles you're used to.'

'What would we have to do to earn it?' Simon said with carefully calculated doubt.

'Play straight with the Guild. They want the material badly, and if we don't trick them we'll be protected by their own rules. And with that much money, there are a hundred places in the galaxy where you'd be safe from High Earth for the rest of your life.'

'And what about your half-sister?'

'Well, I'd be sorry to lose that chance, but cheating the Guild wouldn't bring her back, would it? And in a way, wouldn't it be *aesthetically* more satisfying to pay them back for Jillith by being scrupulously fair with them? "Justice is Love", you know, and all that.'

'I don't know,' Simon said fretfully. 'The difficulty lies in defining justice, I suppose – you know as well as I do that it can excuse the most complicated treasons. And "What do you mean by love?" isn't easily answerable either. In the end one has to chuck it off as a woman's question, too private to be meaningful in a man's world – let alone in matters of polity. Hmmmm.'

This maundering served no purpose but to suggest that Simon was still trying to make up his mind; actually he had reached a decision several minutes ago. Da-Ud had broken; he would have to be disposed of.

Da-Ud listened with an expression of polite bafflement which did not quite completely conceal a gleam of incipient triumph. Ducking a trumpet-vine which appeared to be trying to crown him with thorns, Simon added at last: 'You may well be right – but we'll have to be mortally careful. There may after all be another agent from High Earth here; in matters of this importance they wouldn't be likely to rest with only one charge in the chamber. That means you'll have to follow my instructions to the letter, or we'll never live to spend a riyal of the proceeds.'

'You can count on me,' Da-Ud said, tossing his hair out of his eyes. 'I've handled everything well enough this time, haven't I? And after all it was my idea.'

'Certainly; an expert production. Very well. What I want you to do now is go back to Valkol and tell him that I've betrayed you, and sold the other half of the secret to the Rood-Prince.'

'Surely you wouldn't actually do such a thing!'

'Oh, but I would, and I shall – the deed will be done by the time you get back to Druidsfall, and for the same twenty riyals that you paid for your half.'

'But the purpose – ?'

'Simple. I cannot come to Druidsfall with my remaining half – if there's another Earthman there, I'd be shot before I got half-way up the steps of the Hall. I want the Guild to consolidate the two halves by what seems to be an unrelated act of aggression, between local parties. You make this clear to them by telling them that I won't actually make the sale to the Rood-Prince until I hear from you that you have the rest of the money. To get the point across at once, when you tell His Politeness that I've "betrayed" you – wink.'

'And how do I get word to you this time?'

'You wear this ring. It communicates with a receiver in my Clasp. I'll take matters from there.'

The ring – which was actually only a ring, which would never communicate anything to anybody – changed hands. Then Da-Ud saluted Simon with solemn glee, and went away to whatever niche in history – and in the walls of the Guild hall of Boadicea – is reserved for traitors without style; and Simon, breaking the stalk of a lyre-bush which had sprung up between his feet, went off to hold his muttering, nattering skull and do nothing at all.

Valkol the Polite – or the Exarch's agent, it hardly mattered which – did not waste any time. From a vantage-point high up on the principate's only suitable mountain, Simon watched their style of warfare with appreciation and some wonder.

Actually, in the manoeuvring itself the hand of the Exarchy did not show, and did not need to; for the whole campaign would have seemed like a token display, like a tournament, had it not been for the few score of casualties which seemed inflicted almost inadvertently. Even among these there were not many deaths, as far as Simon could tell – at least, not by the standards of battle to which he was accustomed. Clearly nobody who mattered got killed, on either side.

The Rood-Prince, in an exhibition of bravado more garish than sensible deployed on the plain before his city several thousand pennon-bearing mounted troopers who had nobody to fight but a rabble of foot soldiers which Druidsfall obviously did not intend to be taken seriously; whereupon the city was taken from the Gulf side, by a squadron of flying submarines which broke from the surface of the sea on four buzzing wings like so many dragonflies.

These devices particularly intrigued Simon. Some Boadicious genius, unknown to the rest of the glaxy, had solved the ornithopter problem . . . though the wings were membranous rather than feathered. Hovering, the machines thrummed their wings through a phase shift of a full 180 degrees, but when they swooped the wings moved in a horizontal figure eight, lifting with a forward-and-down stroke, and propelling with the backstroke. A long fish-like tail gave stability, and doubtless had other uses under water.

After the mock battle, the 'thopters landed and the troops withdrew; and then matters took a more sinister turn, manifested by thumping explosions and curls of smoke from inside the Rood palace. Evidently a search was being made for the supposedly hidden documents Simon was thought to have sold, and it was not going well. The sounds of demolition, and the occasional public hangings, could only mean that a maximum interrogation of the Rood-Prince had failed to produce any papers, or any clues to them.

This Simon regretted, as he did the elimination of Da-Ud. He was not normally so ruthless – an outside expert would have called his workmanship in this affair perilously close to being sloppy – but the confusion caused by the transduction serum, now rapidly rising as it approached term, had prevented him from manipulating every factor as subtly as he had originally hoped to do. Only the grand design was still intact now: It would now be assumed that Boadicea had clumsily betrayed the Exarchy leaving the Guild no way out but to capitulate utterly to Simon . . . with whatever additional humiliations he judged might not jeopardize the mission, for Jillith's sake –

Something abruptly cut off his view of the palace. He snatched his binoculars away from his eyes in alarm.

The object that had come between him and the Gulf was a mounted man – or rather, the idiot-headed apteryx the man was sitting on. Simon was surrounded by a ring of them, their lance-points aimed at his chest, pennons trailing in the dusty sareh-grass. The pennons bore the device of the Rood-Prince; but every lancer in the force was a vombis.

Simon rose resignedly, with a token snarl intended more for

himself than for the impassive protean creatures and their fat birds. He wondered why it had never occurred to him before that the vombis might be as sensitive to him as he was to them.

But the answer to that no longer mattered. Sloppiness was about to win its long-postponed reward.

IV

They put him naked into a wet cell: a narrow closet completely clad in yellow alabaster, down the sides of which water oozed and beaded all day long, running out into gutters at the edges. He was able to judge when it was day, because there were clouded bull's-eye lenses in each of the four walls which waxed and waned at him with any outside light; the wet cell was a sort of inverted oubliette, thrust high up into Boadicea's air, probably a hypertrophied merlon on one of the towers of the Traitors' Hall. At night, a fifth lens, backed by a sodium vapour lamp, glared down from the ceiling, surrounded by a faint haze of steam where the dew tried to condense on it.

Escape was a useless fantasy. Erected into the sky as it was, the wet cell did not even partake of the usual character of the building's walls, except for one stain in the alabaster which might have been the under side of a child's footprint; otherwise the veinings were mockingly meaningless. The only exit was down, an orifice through which they had inserted him as though he were being born, and now plugged like the bottom of a stopped toilet. Could he have broken through one of the lenses with his bare hands, he would have found himself naked and torn on the highest point in Druidsfall, with no place to go.

Naked he was. Not only had they pulled all his teeth in search of more poisons, but of course they had also taken his Clasp. He hoped they would fool with the Clasp – it would make a clean death for everybody – but doubtless they had better sense. As for the teeth, they would regrow if he lived, that was one of the few positive advantages of the transduction serum, but in the meantime his bare jaws ached abominably.

They had missed the antidote, which was in a tiny gel capsule in his left earlobe, masquerading as a sebaceous cyst – left, because it is automatic to neglect that side of a man, as though it were only a mirror image of the examiner's right – and that was some comfort. In a few more days now, the gel would dissolve, he would lose his multiple disguise, and then he would have to confess, but in the meantime he could manage to be content despite the slimy glaring cold of the cell.

And in the meantime, he practised making virtues of deficiencies: in this instance, calling upon his only inner resources – the diverting mutterings of his other personalities – and trying to guess what they might once have meant. Some said:

'But I mean, like, you know –'

'Wheah they goin'?'

'Yeah.'

'Led's gehdahda heah – he-he-he!'

'Wheah?'

'So anyway, so uh.'

Others:

'It's hard not to recognize a pigeon.'

'But Mother's birthday is July 20.'

'So he knew that the inevitable might happen –'

'It made my scalp creak and my blood curl.'

'Where do you get those crazy ideas?'

And others:

'Acquit Socrates!'

'Back when she was sure she was married to a window-washer.'

'I don't know what you've got under your skirt, but it's wearing white socks.'

'And then she made a noise like a spindizzy going sour.'

And others:

'Pepe Satan, pepe Satan aleppe.'

'Why, so might any man.'

'EVACUATE MARS!'

'And then she sez to me, she sez –'

' . . . if he would abandon his mind to it.'

'With all of love.'

And . . . but at that point the plug began to unscrew and from the spargers above him which formerly had kept the dampness running, a heavy gas began to curl. They had tired of waiting for him to weary of himself, and the second phase of his questioning was about to begin.

They questioned him, dressed in a hospital gown so worn that it was more starch than fabric, in the Traitor-in-Chief's private office to begin with – a deceptively bluff, hearty, leather-and-piperacks sort of room, which might have been reassuring to a novice. There were only two of them: Valkol in his usual abah, and the 'slave', now dressed as a Charioteer of the high blood. It was a curious choice of costume, since Charioteers were supposed to be free, leaving it uncertain which was truly master and which slave; Simon did not think it could have been Valkol's idea.

Noticing the direction of his glance, Valkol said, 'I asked this gentleman to join me to assure you, should you be in any doubt, that this interview is serious. I presume you know who he is.'

'I don't know who "he" is,' Simon said, with the faintest of emphasis. 'But it must be representing the Green Exarch, since it's a vombis.'

The Traitor-in-Chief's lips whitened slightly. Aha, then he hadn't known that! 'Prove it,' he said.

'My dear Valkol,' the creature interposed. 'Pray don't let him distract us over trifles. Such a thing could not be proved without the most elaborate of laboratory tests, as we all know. And the accusation shows what we wish to know, i.e., that he is aware of who I am – otherwise why try to make such an inflammatory charge?'

'Your master's voice,' Simon said. 'Let us by all means proceed – this gown is chilly.'

'This gentleman,' Valkol said, exactly as if he had not heard any of the four proceeding speeches, 'is Chag Sharance of the Exarchy. Not from the embassy, but directly from the court – he is His Majesty's deputy Fomentor.'

'Appropriate,' Simon murmured.

'We know you now style yourself Simon de Kuyl, but what is more to the point, that you proclaim yourself the Traitor-in-Chief of High Earth. Documents now in my possession persuade me that that if you are not in fact that officer, you are so close to being he as makes no difference. Possibly the man you replaced, the putative amateur with the absurd belt of poison-shells, was actually he. In any event you are the man we want.'

'Flattering of you.'

'Not at all,' said Valkol the Polite. 'We simply want the remainder of those documents, for which we paid. Where are they?'

'I sold them to the Rood-Prince.'

'He had them not, nor could he be persuaded to remember any such transaction.'

'Of course not,' Simon said with a smile. 'I sold them for twenty riyals; do you think the Rood-Prince would recall any such piddling exchange? I appeared as a bookseller, and sold them to his librarian. I suppose you burned the library – barbarians always do.'

Valkol looked at the vombis. 'The price agrees with the, uh, testimony of Da-Ud tam Altair. Do you think – ?'

'It is possible. But we should take no chances; e.g., such a search would be time-consuming.'

The glitter in Valkol's eyes grew brighter and colder. 'True. Perhaps the quickest course would be to give him over to the Sodality.'

Simon snorted. The Sodality was a lay organization to which Guilds classically entrusted certain functions the Guild lacked time and manpower to undertake, chiefly crude physical torture.

'If I'm really who you think I am,' he said, 'such a course would win you nothing but an unattractive cadaver – not even suitable for masonry repair.'

'True,' Valkol said reluctantly. 'I don't suppose you could be induced – politely – to deal fairly with us, at this late date? After all, we did pay for the documents in question, and not any mere twenty riyals.'

'I haven't the money yet.'

'Naturally not, since the unfortunate Da-Ud was held here with it until we decided he no longer had any use for it. However, if upon the proper oaths –'

'High Earth is the oldest oath-breaker of them all,' the Fomentor said. 'We – viz., the Exarchy – have no more time for such trials. The question must be put.'

'So it would seem. Though I hate to handle a colleague thus.'

'You fear High Earth,' the vombis said. 'My dear Valkol, may I remind you – '

'Yes, yes, I know all that,' Valkol snapped to Simon's surprise. 'Nevertheless – Mr de Kuyl, are you *sure* we have no recourse but to send you to the Babble Room?'

'Why not?' Simon said. 'I rather enjoy hearing myself think. In fact, that's what I was doing when you two interrupted me.'

Simon was naturally far from feeling all the bravado he had voiced, but he had no choice left but to trust to the transduction serum, which was now on the shuddering, giddy verge of depriving all three of them of what they each most wanted. Only Simon could know this, but only he also knew something much worse – that in so far as his distorted time-sense could calculate, the antidote was due to be released into his blood-stream at best in another six hours, at worst within only a few minutes. After that, the Exarchy's creature would be the only victor – and the only survivor.

And when he saw the Guild's toposcope laboratory, he wondered if even the serum would be enough to protect him. There was nothing in the least outmoded about it; Simon had never encountered its like even on High Earth. Exarchy equipment, all too probably.

Nor did the apparatus disappoint him. It drove directly down into his subconscious with the resistless unconcern of a spike penetrating a toy balloon. Immediately, a set of loud-speakers above his supine body burst into multi-voiced life:

'Is this some trick? No one but Berentz had a translation-permit – '

'Now the overdrive my-other must woo and win me – '

'Wie schaffen Sie es, solche Entfernungen bei Unterlichtgeschwindigkeit zurueckzulegen?'

'REMEMBER THOR FIVE!'

'Pok. Pok. Pok.'

'We're so tired of wading in blood, so tired of drinking blood, so tired of dreaming about blood –'

The last voice rose to a scream and all the loudspeakers cut off abruptly. Valkol's face, baffled but not yet worried, hovered over Simon's, peering into his eyes.

'We're not going to get anything out of that,' he told some invisible technician. 'You must have gone too deep; those are the archetypes you're getting, obviously.'

'Nonsense.' The voice was the Fomentor's. 'The archetypes sound nothing like that – for which you should be grateful. In any event we have barely gone beneath the surface of the cortex; see for yourself.'

Valkol's face withdrew. 'Hmm. Well, *something's* wrong. Maybe your probe is too broad. Try it again.'

The spike drove home, and the loudspeakers resumed their mixed chorus.

'Nausentampen. Eddettompic. Berobsilom. Aimkaksetchoc. Sanbetogmow—'

'Dîtes-lui que nous lui ordonnons de revenir, en vertu de la Loi du Grand Tout.'

'Perhaps he should swear by another country.'

'Can't Mommy ladder spaceship think for bye-bye-see-you two windy Daddy bottle seconds straight –'

'Nansima macamba yonso cakosilisia.'

'Stars don't have points. They're round, like balls.'

The sound clicked off again. Valkol said fretfully: 'He can't be resisting. You've got to be doing something wrong, that's all.'

Though the operative part of the statement was untrue, it was apparently also inarguable to the Fomentor. There was quite a long silence, broken only occasionally by small hums and clinks.

While he waited, Simon suddenly felt the beginnings of a slow sense of relief in his left earlobe, as though a tiny but unnatural pressure he had long learned to live with had decided to give way, precisely, in fact, like the opening of a cyst.

That was the end. Now he had but fifteen minutes more in which the toposcope would continue to vomit forth its confusion – its steadily diminishing confusion . . . and only an hour before even his physical appearance would reorganize, though that would no longer matter in the least.

It was time to exercise the last option – now, before the probe could by-pass his cortex and again prevent him from speaking his own, fully conscious mind. He said:

'Never mind, Valkol. I'll give you what you want.'

'What? By Gro, I'm not going to give you –'

'You don't have to give me anything, I'm not selling anything. You see for yourself that you can't get to the material with that machine. Not with any other like it, I may add. But I exercise my option to turn my coat, under Guild laws; that gives me safe-conduct, and that's sufficient.'

'No,' the Fomentor's voice said. 'It is incredible – he is in no pain and has frustrated the machine; why should he yield? Besides, the secret of his resistance –'

'Hush,' Valkol said. 'I am moved to ask if you *are* a vombis; doubtless the machine would tell us that much. Mr de Kuyl, I respect the option, but I am not convinced yet. The motive, please.'

'High Earth is not enough,' Simon said. 'Remember Ezra- Tse? "The last temptation is the final treason . . . To do the right thing for the wrong reason." I would rather deal fairly with you, and then begin the long task of becoming honest with myself. But with you only, Valkol – not the Exarchy. I sold the Green Exarch nothing.'

'I see. A most interesting arrangement; I agree. What will you require?'

111

'Perhaps three hours to get myself unscrambled from the effects of fighting your examination. Then I'll dictate the missing material. At the moment it's quite inaccessible.'

' I believe that, too,' Valkol said ruefully. 'Very well –'

'It is not very well,' the vombis said, almost squalling. 'The arrangement is a complete violation of –'

Valkol turned and looked at the creature so hard that it stopped talking of its own accord. Suddenly Simon was sure Valkol no longer needed tests to make up his mind what the Formentor was.

'I would not expect you to understand it,' Valkol said in a very soft voice indeed. 'It is a matter of style.'

Simon was moved to a comfortable apartment and left alone, for well more than the three hours he had asked for. By that time his bodily reorganization was complete, though it would take at least a day for all the residual mental effects of the serum to vanish. When the Traitor-in-Chief finally admitted himself, he made no attempt to disguise either his amazement or his admiration.

'The poison man! High Earth is still a world of miracles. Would it be fair to ask what you did with your, uh, over-populated associate?'

'I disposed of him,' Simon said. 'We have traitors enough already. There is your document; I wrote it out by hand, but you can have a toposcope confirmation whenever you like, now.'

'As soon as my technicians master the new equipment – we shot the monster, of course, though I don't doubt the Exarch will resent it.'

'When you see the rest of the material you may not care what the Exarch thinks,' Simon said. 'You will find that I've brought you a high alliance – though it was Gro's own horns getting it to you.'

'I had begun to suspect as much. Mr de Kuyl – I must assume you are still he, for sanity's sake – that act of surrender was the most elegant gesture I have ever seen. That alone convinced me that you were indeed the Traitor-in-Chief of High Earth and no other.'

'Why, so I was,' Simon said. 'But if you will excuse me now, I think I am about to be somebody else.'

With a mixture of politeness and alarm Valkol left him. It was none too soon. He had a bad taste in his mouth which had nothing to do with his ordeals . . . and, though nobody knew better than he how empty all vengeance is, an inexpungeable memory of Jillith.

Maybe, he thought, 'Justice is Love' after all – not a matter of style, but of spirit. He had expected all these questions to vanish when the antidote took full hold, wiped into the past with the personalities who had done what they had done; but they would not vanish; they were himself.

He had won, but obviously he would never be of use to High Earth again.

In a way, this suited him. A man did not need the transduction serum to be divided against himself. He still had many guilts to accept, and not much left of a lifetime to do it in.

While he was waiting, perhaps he could learn to play the sareh.

SKYSIGN

'*Und ein Schiff mit acht Segeln*
Und mit fünfzig Kanonen
Wird entschwinden mit mir.'
    Pirate-Jenny: *The Threepenny Opera*.

I

Carl Wade came back to consciousness
slowly and with a dull headachy feeling, as though fighting off a
barbiturate hangover – as under the circumstances was quite
possible. He remembered right away that he had been one of the
people who had volunteered to go aboard the alien spaceship
which had been hanging motionless over San Francisco for the
last month. The 'lay volunteer', the Pentagon men had insultingly
called him. And it was likely that the aliens would have drugged
him, because to them, after all, he was only a specimen, and therefore possibly dangerous –

But that didn't seem quite right. Somehow, he could not bring
his memory into focus. He hadn't actually been taken aboard the
ship, as far as he could recall. On the night before he had been
supposed to join the volunteer group, in honour of his own
approaching martyrdom (as he liked to think of it) he and some
friends from the local Hobbit Society, including the new girl, had
cycled up to Telegraph Hill to take a look at the great ship. But
it had only just continued to hang there, showing no lights, no
motion, no activity of any kind except a faint Moon-highlight, as
had been the case ever since it had first popped into view in the
skies over Berkeley – it responded only to the answers to its own
radio messages, only to answers, never to questions – and the
club had quickly gotten bored with it.

And then what? Had they all gone off and gotten drunk? Had
he managed to get the new girl to bed and was now about to have
one of those morning-afters beside her? Or was he in a cell as an
aftermath of a brawl?

114

No one of these ideas evoked any echo in his memory except old ones; and a persistent hunch that he *was* on the spaceship, all the same discouraged him from opening his eyes yet. He wondered what insanity had ever led him to volunteer, and what even greater insanity had led the Pentagon people to choose him over all other saucerites and other space nuts.

A vague clink of sound, subdued and metallic caught his attention. He couldn't identify it, but somehow it sounded surgical. As far as it went, this matched with the quiet around him, the clean coolness of the air, and the unrumpled, also apparently clean pallet he seemed to be lying on. He was neither in a jail nor in the pad of anybody he knew. On the other hand, he didn't feel ill enough to be in hospital ward; just a little drugged. The college infirmary? No, nonsense, he'd been thrown out of college last year.

In short, he *must* be on the ship, simply because this must be the day after yesterday. The thought made him squeeze his eyes still tighter shut. A moment later, further speculation was cut off by a feminine voice, unknown to him, and both pleasantly sexy and unpleasantly self-possessed, but obviously human. It said:

'I see you've given us his language, rather than him ours.'

'It cops out on – rules out – avoids – obviates making everyone else on board guard their tongues,' a man's voice replied. 'Man, I really had to dig for that one. He's got a constipated vocabulary; knows words, but hates them.'

'That's helpful, too,' the woman's voice responded. 'If he can't address himself precisely, it'll matter less what *we* say to him.'

Man, Carl thought, if I ever get that chick where I want her, I'll sell chances on her to wetbacks. But she was still talking:

'But what's he faking for, Brand? He's obviously wide awake.'

At this Carl opened his eyes and mouth to protest indignantly that he wasn't faking, realized his mistake, tried to close both again, and found himself gasping and goggling instead.

He could not see the woman, but the man called Brand was standing directly over him, looking down into his face. Brand looked like a robot – no; remembering the man's snotty remark about his vocabulary, Carl corrected himself: He looked like a fine silver statue, or like a silver version of Talos, the Man of Brass (and wouldn't Carl's damned faculty advisor have been surprised at how fast he'd come up with that one!). The metal shone brilliantly in the blue light of the surgery-like room, but did not look like plate metal. It did not look hard at all. When Brand

115

moved, it flowed with the movement of the muscles under it, like skin.

Yet somehow Carl was dead sure that it wasn't skin, but clothing of some sort. Between the metallic eye-slits, the man's eyes were brown and human, and Carl could even see the faint webbing of blood-vessels in their whites. Also, when he spoke, the inside of his mouth was normal mucous membrane – black like a chow's mouth instead of red, but certainly not metal. On the other hand, the mouth, disconcertingly, vanished entirely when it was closed, and so did the eyes when they clinked; the metal flowed together as instantly as it parted.

'That's better,' the man said. 'Check his responses, Lavelle. He still looks a little dopey. Damn this language.'

He turned away and the woman – her name had certainly sounded like Lavelle – came into view, obviously in no hurry. She was metallic, too, but her metal was black, though her eyes were grey-green. The integument was exceedingly like a skin, yet seeing her Carl was even more convinced that it was either clothing or a body-mask, for there was nothing at all to see where Carl instantly looked. Also, he noticed a moment later, either she had had no hair or else her skull cap – if that was what she wore – was very tight, a point that hadn't occurred to him while looking at the man.

She took Carl's pulse, and then looked expertly under his upper eyelids. 'Slight fugue, that's all,' she said with a startling pink flash of tongue. Yet not quite so startling as Brand's speaking had been, since a pink mouth in a black face was closer to Carl's experience than was any sort of mouth in a silver face. 'He can go down to the cages any time.'

Cages?

'Demonstration first,' Brand, now out of sight again, said in an abstracted voice. Carl chanced moving his head slightly and found that his horizon headache was actually a faint one-side earache, which made no sense to him at all. The movement also showed him the dimensions of the room, which was no larger than an ordinary living room – maybe 12' by 13' – and painted an off-white. There was also some electronic apparatus here and there, but no more than Carl had seen in the pads of some hi-fi bugs he knew, and to his eyes not much more interesting. In a corner was a drop-down bunk, evidently duplicating the one he now occupied. Over an oval metal door – the only ship-like feature he could see – was a dial-face like that of a huge barometer or clock, its figures too small to read from where he lay, and much too closely spaced too.

Brand reappeared. After a moment, the shining black woman called Lavelle took up a position a few feet behind him and to his left.

'I want to show you something,' the man said to Carl. 'You can see just by looking at us that it would do you no good to jump us – to attack us. Do you dig – do you understand that?'

'Sure,' Carl said, rather more eagerly than he had intended. As a first word, it wasn't a very good one.

'All right.' Brand put both his hands on his hips, just below his waist, and seemed to brace himself slightly. 'But there's a lot more to it than you see at the moment. Watch closely.'

Instantly the silver man and Lavelle changed places. It happened so suddenly and without any transition that for a second Carl failed to register what he was supposed to have noticed. Neither of the two metal people had moved in the slightest. They were just each one standing where the other one had been standing before.

'Now – ' the man said.

At once, he was back where he had been, but the gleaming black woman – man, that outfit was sexy! – was standing far back, by the oval door. Again, there'd been not a whisper or hint of any motion in the room.

'And once more –'

This time the result was much more confusing. The metal aliens seemed to have moved, but after a while Carl realized that they hadn't; *he* had. The switch was so drastic that for an instant he had thought they – all three of them – were in another room; even the hands of the dial-face looked changed. But actually, all that had happened was that he was now in the other bunk.

The switch made hash of a hypotheses he had only barely begun to work out: that the metal skins or suits made it possible for Brand and Lavelle to swap places, or jump elsewhere at will, by something like teleportation. If that was how it worked, then Carl might just hook one of those shiny suits, and then, *flup*! and –

– and without benefit of suit white or black, he was in the other bunk, huddled in the ruins of his theory and feeling damned scared. On the face of a cathode-ray oscilloscope now in his field of view, a wiggly green trace diagrammed pulses which he was sure showed exactly how scared he was; he had always suspected any such instrument of being able to read his mind. The suspicion turned to rage and humiliation when Lavelle looked at the

117

machine's display and laughed, in a descending arpeggio, like a coloratura soprano.

'He draws the moral,' she said.

Wetbacks. Also King Kong, if possible.

'Possibly,' said the silver man. 'We'll let it go for now, anyhow. It's time for the next subject. You can get up now.'

This last sentence seemed to be addressed to Carl. He stiffened for a moment, half expecting either the metal people or the room – or perhaps himself – to vanish, but since nothing at all changed, he slid cautiously to his feet.

Looking down at the feet, and on upward from there as far as he could without seeming vain about it, he discovered that he was wearing the same scuffed sneakers and soiled slacks he had been wearing when he had gone cycling with the Hobbit crowd, except that both the clothing and his own self under it had been given a thorough bath. He was offended by that discovery, but at the moment not very much. Did it mean that there really had been *no* events between that expedition to Telegraph Hill, and this nightmare?

'Am I on the ship?' he said. It was a difficult sentence to get out.

'Of course,' said the silver man.

'But I never got to join the official party – or I don't think –'

'Nobody will come aboard with the official party, Jack. We selected the few we wanted from among the cats your people designated. The rest will cool their heels.'

'Then what am I –'

'Too many answers,' Lavelle said.

'Never mind,' said the silver man. 'It won't matter for long, chicklet. Come along Mister – Wade? – yes; we'll interview you later, and answer some of your questions then, if we feel up to it. Lavelle, stay here and set up for the next live one. And Mister Wade, one other thing, should you feel ambitious, just bear in mind –'

The metal-skinned people changed places, silently, instantly, without the slightest preparation, without the slightest follow-through.

'– that we're a little faster on the draw than you are,' Brand finished from his new position, evenly, but his voice smiting Carl's other ear like a final insult. 'We need no other weapons. Dig me?'

'Yulp,' Carl said. As a final word, it was not much better than his first.

The sheathed man led him out of the oval door.

118

II

Numb as he had thought he was by now to everything but his own alarm, Carl was surprised to be surprised by the spaciousness of what they had called 'the cages'. His section of them reminded him more of an executive suite, or his imaginings of one – a large single bedroom, a wardrobe, a bathroom, and a sort of office containing a desk with a small T.V screen and a headset like a cross between a hair-drier and a set of noise-mufflers.

He had been marched to this in total silence by the silver man, through a long corridor where they had passed several others of the metal people, all of whom had passed them by wordlessly and with their eyes as blanked out as Little Orphan Annie's. Once they had arrived at the cage, however, Brand had turned affable, showing him the facilities, even including a stock of clean clothes and seating him at last at the desk.

'I'll talk to you further when there's more time,' the silver man said. 'At the moment we're still recruiting. If you want food, you can call for it through that phone. I hope you know that you can't get away. If you cut out of the cage, there'd be no place where you could wind up.'

Brand reached forward to the desk and touched something. Under Carl's feet, a circular area about the size of a snow-slider turned transparent, and Carl found himself looking down at the Bay area through nothing but ten miles or more of thin air. Even moderate heights had always made him sick; he clutched at the edge of the desk and was just about to lose his option when the floor turned solid again.

'I wanted you to see,' Brand said, 'that you really are aboard our ship. By the way, if you'd like to look through there again, the button for it's right here.'

'Thanks,' Carl said, calling up one of his suavist witticisms, 'but no thanks.'

'Suit yourself. Is there anything else you'd like until we meet again?'

'Well . . . you said you were bringing more, uh, Earth people up here. If you could bring my wife . . . ?'

The answer to this was only of academic interest to Carl. He had been separated from Bea for more than a year, ever since the explosion about college; and on the whole it had been painless, since they had been civilized enough to have been married in the first place only at common law and that a little bit by accident.

119

But it would have been nice to have had someone he knew up here, if only somebody with a reasonably pink skin. The silver man said:

'Sorry. None of the other males we expect to bring aboard will know you, or each other. We find it better to follow the same rule with females, so we won't have any seizures of possessiveness.'

He got up and moved toward the door, which was the usual shape for doors, not oval like the last one. He still seemed relatively gracious, but at the door he turned and added:

'We want you to understand from the outset that up here, you own nobody – and nobody owns you but us.' And with that, in a final silent non-explosion of arrogance, he flicked into nothingness, leaving Carl staring with glazed eyes at the unbroached door.

Of course no warning could have prevented Carl, or anyone else above the mental level of a nematode, from trying to think about escape; and Carl, because he had been selected as the one lay volunteer to visit the spaceship possibly because he had thought about spaceships now and then or read about them, thought he ought to be able to work out some sort of plan – if only he could stop jittering for a few minutes. In order to compose his mind, he got undressed and into the provided pyjamas – the first time he had worn such an outfit in ten years – and ordered the ship (through the desk phones) to send him a bottle of muscatel, which arrived promptly out of a well in the centre of the desk. To test the ship's good will, he ordered five more kinds of drinks, and got them all, some of which he emptied with conscious self-mastery down the toilet.

Then he thought, jingling a luxurious bourbon-and-ginger abstractedly; the sound of ice was peculiarly comforting. Why the hell *had* the Pentagon people picked him as the 'lay volunteer', out of so many? The alien ship had asked for a sampling of human beings to go back to its far star, and of these, it had wanted one to be a man of no specialities whatsoever – or no specialities that the ship had been willing to specify. The Pentagon had picked its own samplings of experts, who probably had been ordered to 'volunteer'; but the 'lay volunteer' had been another matter.

Like everyone else, Carl had been sure the Pentagon would want the 'lay volunteer' actually to be a master spy among all possible master spies, not a James Bond but a Leamas type, a man who could pass for anything; but it hadn't worked that way. Instead, the Pentagon had approved Carl, one slightly beat and more than slightly broke dropout, who believed in magic and the possibility of spaceships, but – leave us face it, monsters and gents – didn't seem to be of much interest either to alien or to human otherwise.

Why, for instance, hadn't the 'lay volunteer' the aliens wanted turned out to be a Bircher, a Black Muslim, a Communist or a Rotarian – in short, some kind of fanatic who purported to deal with the *real* world – instead of a young man who was fanatic only about imaginary creatures called hobbits? Even the ordinary science-fiction fan would have been better; why was a sword-and-sorcery addict required to try to figure his way out of a classical spaceship clink?

Gradually, he began to feel – with pain, and only along the edges – that there was an answer to that. He got up and began to pace, which took him into the bedroom. Once there, he sat down nervously on the bed.

At once, the lights went out. Wondering if he had inadvertently sat on a trigger, he stood up again; but the darkness persisted.

Were the metal people reading his mind again – and trying to suppress any further thinking? It might work. He was damn-all tired, and he'd been out of practice at thinking anyhow. Well, he could lie down and pretend to be asleep. Maybe that would –

The lights went on.

Though he was dead sure that he hadn't fallen asleep, he knew that he was rested. He remembered that when he had looked down the sink-hole under the desk, lights had been coming on around the Bay. Gritting his teeth and swallowing to keep down the anticipated nausea, he went out to the desk and touched the button.

One glance was enough, luckily. It was high morning on Earth. A night had passed.

And what was the thought he had lost? He couldn't remember. The ship had finessed him – as easily as turning a switch.

III

He ordered breakfast; the ship delivered it. The bottles and glasses, he noticed, had been taken away. As an insulting aftermath, the ship also ran him another bath without his having ordered it. He took it, since he saw nothing to be gained by going dirty up here; it would be as unimpressive as carrying a

121

poster around that sink-hole. No razor was provided; evidently the ship didn't object to his beard.

He then went after a cigarette, couldn't find any, and finally settled for a slow burn, which was easy enough to muster from all his deprivations, but somehow wasn't as satisfying as usual. *I'll show them*, he thought; but show them what? They looked invulnerable – and besides, he had no idea what they wanted him for; all the official clues had been snatched away, and no substitutes provided.

How about making a play for Lavelle? *That* would show that chrome-plated s.o.b. But how to get to her? And again, show him what? Carl knew nothing about these people's sexual taboos; they might just not give a damn, like most Earth people on a cruise. And besides, the girl seemed pretty formidable. But lush; it would be fun to break her down. He'd been through stuffier chicks in his time: Bea, for instance, or – well, Bea, for instance. And the separation hadn't really been his fault –

His stomach twinged and he got up to pace. The trouble was that he had nothing to impress Lavelle with but his build, which really wasn't any better than Brand's. His encyclopedic knowledge of the habits of hobbits wasn't going to crush any buttercups around here, and he doubted that being able to sing *Fallout Blues* in two separate keys would, either. Dammit, they'd left him nothing to work with! It was unfair.

Abruptly remembering last night's drinks, he stopped at the desk and tried asking for cigarettes. They materialized instantly. Well, at least the aliens weren't puritans – that was hopeful. Except that he didn't want a complaisant Lavelle; that wouldn't show anybody anything, least of all himself. There was no particular kick in swingers.

But if they gave him drinks and butts, they might just let him roam about, too. Maybe there was somebody else here that he could use, or some other prisoner who could give him clues. For some reason the thought of leaving the cage sparked a brief panic, but he smothered it by thinking of the ship as a sort of convention hotel, and tried the door.

It opened as readily as the entrance to a closet. He paused on the threshold and listened, but there was absolutely no sound except the half expected hum of machinery. Now the question was, supposing the opening of the door had been an accident, and he was not supposed to be prowling around the ship? But that was their worry, not his; they had no right to expect him to obey their rules. Besides, as Buck Rogers used to say under similar circumstances, there was only one way to find out.

There was no choice of direction, since the corridor's ends were both unknown. Moving almost soundlessly – one real advantage of tennis shoes – he padded past a succession of cage doors exactly like his own, all closed and with no clues for guessing who or what lay behind them. Soon, however, he became aware that the corridor curved gently to the right; and just after the curve passed a blind point, he found himself on the rim of a park.

Startled, he shrank back, then crept forward still more cautiously. The space down the ramp ahead was actually a long domed hall or auditorium, oval in shape, perhaps five city blocks in length and two across at the widest point, which was where the opening off the corridor debouched. It seemed to be about ten stories high at the peak, floored with grass and shrubbery, and rimmed with small identical patios – one of which, he realized with a dream-like lack of surprise, must back up against his own cage. It all reminded him unpleasantly of one of those enlightened zoos in which animals are allowed to roam in spurious freedom in a moated 'ecological setting'.

As he looked down into the park, there was a long sourceless sigh like a whisper of metal leaves, and doors opened at the back of each patio. Slowly, people began to come out – pink people, not metal ones. He felt a brief mixture of resentment and chagrin; had he stayed in his own cage, he would have been admitted to the park automatically now, without having had to undergo the jumpy and useless prowl down the companionway.

Anyway, he had found fellow prisoners, just as he had hoped; and it would be safer down there than up here. He loped eagerly downhill.

The ramp he was following ran between two patios. One of them was occupied by a girl, seated upon a perfectly ordinary chair and reading. He swerved, braking.

'Well, hi there!' he said.

She looked up, smiling politely but not at all as pleased to see another inmate as he could have hoped. She was small, neat and smoky, with high cheekbones and black hair – perhaps a Latin Indian, but without the shyness he usually counted upon with such types.

'Hello,' she said. 'What have they got you in for?'

That he understood; it was a standard jailhouse question.

'I'm supposed to be the resident fantasy fan,' he said, in an unusual access of humility. 'Or that's my best guess. My name's Carl Wade. Are you an expert?'

'I'm Jeanette Hilbert. I'm a meteorologist. But as a reason for my being here, it's obviously a fake – this place has about as much weather as a Zeppelin hangar. Apparently it's the same story with all of us.'

'How long have you been here?'

'Two weeks, I think. I wouldn't swear to it.'

'So long? I was snatched only last night.'

'Don't count on it,' Jeanette said. 'Time is funny here. These metal people seem to jump all around in it – or else they can mess with your memory at will.'

Carl remembered the change in the clock face, back when Brand and Lavelle had been showing off their powers for him. It hadn't occurred to him that time rather than space might have been involved, despite that clue. He wished he had read more Hubbard – something about transfer of *theta* from one MEST entity to another – no, he couldn't recapture the concept, which he had never found very illuminating anyhow. Korzybski? Madame Blavatsky? The hell with it. He said:

'How'd you come on board?'

'Suddenly. It was taken right out of my apartment, a day after NASA volunteered me. Woke up in an EEG lab here, having my brain-prints taken.'

'So did I. Hmm. Any fuzzy period between?'

'No, but that doesn't prove anything.' She looked him over, slowly and deliberately. It was not an especially approving glance. 'Is that what fantasy fans usually wear?'

He was abruptly glad that his levis and shirt were at least clean, no matter how willy-nilly. 'Work clothes,' he explained.

'Oh. What kind of work?'

'Photography,' he said, masking a split-second's groping with his most winning smile. It was, he knew, a workable alias; most girls dream of posing. 'But they didn't bring my cameras and stuff along with me, so I guess I'm as useless as you are, really.'

'Oh,' she said, getting up, 'I'm not sure I'm so useless. I didn't bring my barometer, but I still have my head.'

Dropping her book on the chair, she swung away and went back into her cage, moving inside her simple dress as flexibly as a reed.

124

'Hey, Jeanette – I didn't mean – just a – '

Her voice came back: 'They close the doors again after an hour.' Then, as if in mockery, her own door closed behind her, independently.

For want of anything else to do, he stepped into the patio and picked up the book. It was called *Experimental Design*, by one Sir Ronald Fisher, and the first sentence that he hit read: 'In fact, the statement can be made that the probability that the unknown mean of the population is less than a particular limit, is exactly P, namely $Pr\,(u < x + ts) = P$ for all values of P, where t is known (and has been tabulated as a function of P and N).' He dropped the thin volume hastily. He had been wondering vaguely whether Jeanette had brought the book with her or the ship had supplied it, but suddenly he couldn't care less. It began to look as though all the chicks he encountered on this ship had been born to put him down.

Disappointed at his own indifference, he remembered her warning, and looked quickly back at the top of the gangway down which he had come. It was already closed. Suppose he was cut off? There were people down there in the park that he still wanted to talk to – but obviously not now. He raced along the esplanade.

He identified his own cage almost entirely by intuition, and it seemed that he was scarcely in it five minutes before the door to the patio slid shut. Now he had something else to think about, and he was afraid to try it, not only because it was painful, but because despite Jeanette's theories about time and memory, he still thought it very likely that Lavelle and her consort could read his mind. Experience, after all, supported all three theories indifferently, thus far.

But what about the *other* door? Increasingly it seemed to him that he hadn't been intended to go through it. He had been told that he couldn't get out of his cage; and the one hour's access to the park was nothing more than admission to a larger cage, not any sort of permission to roam. The unlocked outer door had to have been an accident. And if so, and if it were still open, there should still be all sorts of uses he might make of it –

He froze, waiting to be jumped into the next day by the mind-readers. Nothing happened. Perhaps they could read his mind, but weren't doing it at the moment. They couldn't be reading everybody's mind ever minute of the day; they were alien and powerful, but also very obviously human in many important ways. All right. Try the outer door again. There was really nothing in the world that he wanted to do less, but the situation was beginning to make him mad, and rage was the only substitute he had for courage.

And after all, what could they do to him if they caught him, besides knock him out? The hell with them. Here goes.

Once more, the door opened readily.

IV

The corridor was as eventless as ever; the ramp to the park now closed. He continued along the long smooth curve, which obviously skirted the park closely, just outside the cage doors. Once he stopped to lay his ear to one of the cages. He heard nothing, but he did notice a circle with a pattern of three holes in it, like a diagram of a bowling ball, just where the lock to an ordinary door would be placed for someone of Brand's height.

That made him think again as he prowled. So the metal people needed handles and locks! Then they couldn't jump about in space as magically as they wanted you to think they could. Whatever the trick was, it wasn't teleportation or time-travel. It was an illusion, or something else to do with the mind, as both Carl and Jeanette had guessed: memory-blanking, or mind-reading. But which?

After he had crept along for what seemed like a mile, the elliptical pathway inflected and began to broaden. Also there was a difference in the quality of the light up ahead: it seemed brighter, and, somehow, more natural. The ceiling was becoming higher, too. He was coming into a new kind of area; and for some reason he did not stop to examine – perhaps only that the inside curve of the corridor was on his right, which as evidence was good for nothing – he felt that he was coming up on the front of the ship.

He had barely begun to register the changes when the corridor put forth a pseudopod: a narrow, shallow, metal stairway which led up to what looked like the beginning of a catwalk, off to the left. He detoured instinctively – in the face of the unknown, hide and peek!

As he went along the outward-curving catwalk, the space ahead of him continued to grow bigger and more complicated, and after a few minutes he saw that his sensation that he was going bowwards had been right. The catwalk ran up and around a large chamber, shaped like a fan opened from this end, and ending in

126

an immense picture window through which daylight poured over a cascade of instruments. On the right side of the room was a separate, smaller bank of controls, divided into three ranks of buttons each arranged in an oval, and surmounted by a large clock-face like the one Carl had noticed when he first awoke in the ship's EEG room. The resemblance to the cockpit of a jet-liner, writ large, was unmistakable; this was the ship's control room.

But there was something much more important to see. Brand – or someone almost exactly like him – was sitting in one of two heavy swivel seats in front of the main instrument board, his silver skin scattering the light from the window into little wavelets all over the walls to either side of him. Occasionally he leaned forward and touched something, but in the main he did not seem to have much to do at the moment. Carl had the impression that he was waiting, which the little flicks of motion only intensified – like a cat watching a rubber mouse.

Carl wondered how long he had been there. From the quality of the light, the time was now either late morning or early after-noon – it was impossible to guess which, since Carl could not read the alien clock.

A movement to the right attracted both men's attention. It was a black metalled woman: Lavelle. Of this identification Carl was dead sure, for he had paid much closer attention to her than to her consort. Lifting a hand in greeting, she came forward and sat down in the other chair, and the two began to talk quietly, their conversation interspersed with occasional bursts of low laughter which made Carl uncomfortable for some reason he did not try to analyse. Though he could catch frequent strings of syllables and an occasional whole sentence, the language was not English, Spanish or French, the only ones he was equipped to recognize; but it was quite liquid, unlike a Germanic or Slavic tongue. Ship's language, he was certain.

Their shadows grew slowly longer on the deck; then it must be afternoon. That double prowl up the corridor must have taken longer than he had thought. He was just beginning to feel hungry when there was a change that made him forget his stomach completely.

As the metal people talked, their voices had been growing quieter and a little more husky. Now, Brand leaned forward and touched the board again, and instantly, like flowers unfolding in stop-motion photography, the metal suits – aha, they *were* suits! –

127

unpeeled around them and seemed to dissolve into the chairs, leaving them both entirely nude.

Now would be the time to jump them, except that he was quite certain he couldn't handle both of them. Instead, he simply watched, grateful for the box seat. There was something about the girl besides her nudity that was disquieting, and after a while Carl realized what it was. Except for her baldness, she bore a strong resemblance to the first girl he had ever made time with by pretending to be a photographer, a similarity emphasized by the way she was sitting in the chair.

Obviously the pose was not lost on Brand either. He got to his feet with a lithe motion, and seizing her hand pulled her to her feet. She went to him freely enough, but after a moment struggled away, laughing, and pointing at the smaller control board, the one with the clock. Brand made an explosive remark, and then, grinning, strode over to the board and

the room was dark and empty. Blinking amazedly, Carl tried to stir, and found that his muscles were completely cramped as if he had been lying on the metal edge in the same position all night.

Just like that, he had the key in his hands.

He began to work out the stiffness slowly, starting with fingers and toes, and surveying the control room while he did so. The room was not really completely dark; there were many little stars gleaming on the control boards, and a very pale dawn was showing through the big window. The large hand on the clock face had jumped a full ninety degrees widdershins.

When he felt ready to take on a fight if he had to – except for his hunger, about which he could do nothing – Carl went back to the stairs and down into the control room, going directly to the smaller of the two boards. There was no doubt in his mind now about what those three ovals of buttons meant. If there was any form of dialogue he understood no matter what the language, it was the dialogue of making out. As plain as plain, the last two lines the denuded metal people had spoken had gone like this:

LAVELLE: But suppose somebody (my husband, the captain, the doctor, the boss) should come in?

BRAND: Oh hell, I'll (lock the door, take the phone off the hook, put out the lights) fix that!

Blackout.

What Brand had done was to put everyone on board to sleep. Out of the suits, he and Lavelle must have been immune to whatever effect he had let loose, so they could play their games at leisure. A neat trick; Carl wouldn't mind learning it – and he thought he was about to.

Because Carl himself was awake now, it was pretty clear that the other prisoners were also; maybe they had been freed automatically by the passage of the clock past a certain point in the morning, and would be put back to sleep just as automatically after supper. It also seemed clear that for the prisoners, the effect didn't depend upon wearing one of the metal suits or being in the cages, since Carl had been knocked out up on the catwalk, almost surely unsuspected. The suits must be the captain's way of controlling the crew – and that meant that Brand (or Brand and Lavelle) must run the shop, since this board was too powerful to allow just anybody to fool with it. Carl rubbed his hands together.

One of these three circles must represent the crew; another, the cages; the third – well, there was no telling who was controlled by those buttons – maybe crew and prisoners at once. But the oval in the middle had the fewest number of buttons, so it was probably a safe bet that it controlled the cages. But how to test that?

Taking a deep breath, Carl systematically pressed each and every button on the left-hand oval. Nothing happened. Since he himself was not now sprawled upon the deck, unconscious again, he could now assume that the crew was once more fast asleep – with the unavoidable exception of any, who had been out of their suits, like the lovers.

Now for the sparser oval. Trying to remind himself that he now had plenty of time, Carl worked out by painful memory and counting upon his fingers just where the button which represented his cage probably was. Then, starting one button away from it, he went again all around the circle until he was one button on the opposite side of what he thought was his own.

It took him a long time, sweating to work himself up to touching either of those two bracketting buttons, but at last, holding his breath, he pressed them both at once, watching the clock as he did so.

He did not fall and the clock did not jump.

The ship was his.

He was not in the slightest doubt about what he was going to do with it. He had old scores by the millions to pay off, and was going to have himself one hell of a time doing it, too. With an instrument like this, no power on Earth could stop him.

Of course he'd need help: somebody to figure out the main

129

control board with him, somebody with a scientific mind and some technical know-how, like Jeanette. But he'd pick his help damn carefully.

The thought of Jeanette made him feel ugly, a sensation he rather enjoyed. She'd been damn snippy. There might be other women in the cages too; and the aborted scene of last night in the control room had left him feeling more frustrated that usual. All right; some new scores, and then he'd get around to the old ones.

V

It was high morning when he got back to the control room. but still it was earlier than he'd expected it to be. There hadn't been many women in the cages, but either they got less and less attractive as he went along, or the recent excitement and stress had taken more out of him physically than he'd realized. Otherwise he was sure he could have completed such a programme handily, maybe even twice around. Oh well, there was plenty of time. Now he needed help.

The first thing to do was to disconnect the clock in some way. That proved to be easy: a red bar under it simply stopped it. Since nobody, obviously, had visited the control room since his last tampering, he now had the whole ship in permanent coma.

Next, he counted down to Jeanette's button and pushed it. That ought to awaken her. The only remaining problem was to work out how that three-hole lock on her cage worked.

That didn't turn out to be easy at all. It took an hour of fumbling before it suddenly sank inward under his hand and the door slid back.

Jeanette was dressed, and stared at him with astonishment.

'How did you do that?' she said. 'What's wrong with the phone Where's the food? Have you been doing something stupid?'

He was just about to lash back at her when he realized that this was no time to start the breaking-off routine, and instead put on his best master-of-the-situation smile, as if he were just starting up with her.

'Not exactly,' he said. 'But I've got control of the ship. Mind if I come in?'

'Control of the ship? But – well, all right, come in. You're in anyhow.'

He came forward and sat down at her version of his desk. She backed away from him, only a little, but quite definitely.

130

'Explain yourself,' she said.

He didn't; but he told her the rudiments of the story, in as earnest and forthright a manner as he had ever managed to muster in his life. As he had expected, she asked sharp technical questions, most of which he parried, and her superior manner dissolved gradually into one of intense interest.

All the same, whenever he made the slightest movement to stand up, she stepped lightly away from him, a puzzled expression flitted across her face and then vanished again as he fed her new details. He was puzzled in turn. Though the enforced ship's-sleep hadn't prevented her from being highly responsive – in fact, it was his guess that it had helped – he was sure that she had never awoken even for a second during the morning and hence had nothing to blame him for. Yet it was obvious that she knew, somewhere in the back of her mind that *something* had happened to her, and associated it with him. Well, maybe that would be helpful too, in the long run; a cut cake goes stale in a hurry.

When he was through, she said reluctantly: 'That was close observation, and quick thinking.'

'Not very quick. It took me all morning to work it out.'

Again the flitting, puzzling expression. 'You got the right answer in time. That's as quick as anybody needs to be. Did you wake anybody else?'

'No just you. I don't know anybody else here, and I figured you could help me. Besides, I didn't want a mob of released prisoners running around the ship kicking the crew and fooling with things.'

'Hmm. Also sensible. I must say, you surprise me.' Carl couldn't resist a grin at this, but took care to make it look bashful. 'Well – what do you suggest we do now?'

'We ought to figure out the main control board. See if it's possible for us to run the ship without anybody from the crew to help – and how many hands from the cages we'd need to do the job.'

'Yes,' she said thoughtfully. 'At a guess, the main control board is as rational as the sleep-board is. And the two captains – Brand and Lavelle – must be able to run the ship from there all by themselves in a pinch; otherwise the threat of knocking all the rest of the crew out wouldn't have sufficient force. Interesting social system these people must have. I don't think I like them.'

'Me neither,' Carl said with enthusiasm. 'I hate people who whip serfs.'

Jeanette's eyebrows rose. 'The crew can't be serfs. They wear

131

the metal suits – a powerful tool in any hands – and can take them off whenever they like if they want to duck the sleep-compulsion. But obviously they don't. They can't be serfs; they must be something like chattel slaves, who'd never dream of changing status except to other owners. But that's not nearly the most interesting problem.'

'What is, then?'

'How the buttons put *us* to sleep. We don't wear the suits.'

Since this was the problem Carl most badly wanted to solve secretly and for himself alone, it was the one he most badly wanted Jeanette not to think about; yet since he had no clues at all, he had to chance at least a tentative sounding before trying to divert her from it. He said: 'Any ideas?'

'Not at the first moment. Hmm . . . Did you have a headache when you first woke up on board?'

'I've got it still,' he said, patting the back of his neck tenderly. 'Why? Does that signify?'

'Probably not. I'll just have to look at the board, that's all. We'd better go take a thorough look around.'

'Sure. This way.'

She was very thorough – exasperatingly so. Long after he would have been sure that he had seen everything, she would return to some small instrument complex she had looked at three or four times before, and go over it again as if she had never seen it before. She volunteered nothing except an occasional small puff of surprise or interest; and to his questions, she replied uniformly, 'I don't know yet.' Except once when after she had bent over a panel of travelling tapes for what must have been twenty minutes, she had said instead, 'Shut up for ten seconds, will you?'

In the meantime, the sun was reddening towards afternoon again, and Carl was becoming painfully conscious of the fact that he had had nothing to eat since breakfast the day before. Every minute added without any food shortened his temper, reduced his attention span and cut into his patience. Maybe the girl was getting results, and maybe not, but he was more and more sure that she was putting him on. Didn't she know who was boss here?

Maybe she thought she could make a dash for the sleep-panel and turn *him* off. If she tried that, he would knock her down. He had never been that far away from the panel; he was on guard.

Suddenly she straightened from the main board and sat down in one of the heavy swivel chairs. It promptly began to peel her

132

clothes off. Though he had not told her anything about this trick, she got up quickly so that it left her only slightly shredded around the edges. She eyed the chair thoughtfully, but said nothing. For some reason this was her most galling silence of all.

'Got anything?' he said harshly.

'Yes, I think so. These controls require an optimum of three people, but two can run them in an emergency. Ordinarily I think they use five, but two of those must be standbys.'

'Could one man handle them?'

'Not a chance. There are really three posts here: pilot, engineer, navigator. The pilot and the navigator can be the same person if it's absolutely necessary. Nobody can substitute for the engineer. This ship runs off a Nernst-effect generator, a very tricky form of hydrogen fusion. The generators idle very nicely, but when they're drawing real power they have to be watched – more than that, it takes a real musician's hand to play them.'

'Could you do it?'

'I'd hate to try. Maybe with a month of ant-steps, saying "May I" all the way. But if the thing blew at this altitude it'd take out the whole West Coast – at a minimum. There's an awful lot of hydrogen in the Pacific; I wouldn't answer for what a Nernst fireball would really start.'

'Good.'

She swung on him, her brows drawing together. 'What's good about it? What are you up to, anyhow?'

'Nothing very awful,' he said, trying to be placating. 'I'll tell you in a minute. First of all, have you figured out how to get the grub moving again? I'm starving.'

'Yes, that's what the third oval on the sleep board is – the phone system locks. There's a potentiometer system on the side of the board that chooses what's activated – food, phones, doors, and so on. If you'll move over a minute, I'll show you.'

'In a minute,' he said. 'It's not that I don't trust you, Jeanette, but you know how it is – now that I've got my mitts on this thing I hate to let go of it.'

'That figures. What are you going to do with it?'

'I don't know till I've got it doped better. First, how about this business of putting the prisoners crumped without any suits?'

'No,' she said.

'Whadd'ya mean, no?' he said, feeling the ugliness rise again. 'Listen, chick –'

He caught himself, but with an awful feeling that it was too

133

late. She watched him damping himself down with sober amusement, and then said:

'Go on. That was the true hyena laugh.'

He clenched his fists, and again fought himself back to normal, aware that she was observing every step of the process.

He said:

'I'm sorry. I'm tired and hungry. I'll try not to snarl at you again. Okay?'

'Okay.' But she said nothing more.

'So what about this crump effect?'

'Sorry I won't answer any more questions until you've answered one of mine. It's very simple. Once you've really got control of the ship – and you can't get it without me – what do you plan to do with it? You keep telling me you'll tell me "in a minute". Tell me now.'

'All right,' he said, his teeth on edge. 'All right. Just remember that you asked me for it. If you don't like it, tough tibby – it's not my fault. I'm going to use this ship and everybody on it to set things straight. The warmongers, the blue-noses, the fuzz, the snobs, the squares, the bureaucrats, the Uncle Toms, the Birchers, the Fascists, the rich-bitches, the . . . everybody who's ever been *against* anything is going to get it now, right in the neck. I'm going to tear down all the vested interests, from here to Tokyo. If they go along with me, okay. If they don't, blooey! If I can't put them to sleep I can blow 'em up. I'm going to strike out for freedom for *everybody*, in all directions, and all at once. There'll never be a better chance. There'll never be a better weapon than this ship. And there'll never be a better man than me to do it.'

His voice sank slightly. The dream was catching hold. 'You know damn well what'd happen if I let this ship get taken over by the Pentagon or the fuzz. They'd suppress it – hide it – make a weapon out of it. It'd make the cold war worse. And the sleep gadget – they'd run all our lives with it. Sneak up on us. Jump in and out of our pads. Spy. All the rest. Right now's our chance to do justice with it. And that by God is what I'm going to do with it!'

'Why you?' Jeanette said. Her voice sounded very remote.

'Because I know what the underdog goes through. I've gone through it all. I've been put down by every kind of slob that walks the Earth. And I've got a long memory. I remember every one of them. Every one. In my mind, every one of them has a front name, a hind name, and an address. With a thing like this ship, I can

134

track every man jack of them down and pay them off. No exceptions. No hiding. No mercy... just justice. The real, pure simple thing.'

'Sounds good.'

'You bet it's good!'

'What about the Soviets? I missed them on your list, somehow.'

'Oh sure; I hate Communists. And also the militarists – it was the Pentagon that sucked us into this mess up here to begin with, you know that. Freedom for everybody – at one stroke!'

She seemed to consider that. 'Women, too?'

'Of course, women! The hell with the double standard! On both sides!'

'I don't quite follow you,' she said. 'I thought the double standard only had one side – the men could and the women couldn't.'

'You know damn well that's not so. It's the women who control the situation – they always can, they're the ones who get to say *no*. The real freedom is all on their side.'

'How'd you fix that?' she said, in a voice almost sleepy.

'I... well, I haven't had much of a chance to think about it –'

'I think you've thought about it quite a lot.'

Her shredded dress trailing streamers, Jeanette walked steadily away from the control board toward the corridor. Carl put his finger over her button.

'Stop!'

She stopped and turned, shielding her thighs with one hand in a peculiarly modest gesture, considering everything.

'Well?'

'I don't give a damn what you think. If you don't dig it, that's your nuisance – sorry about that, Chief. But I need you; I'll have you.'

'No you won't. You can put me to sleep and rape me, but you won't have me.'

'Yes I will. I can wake you up. And I won't feed you. You'll spend the rest of your time in your cage – hungry and wide awake. In the meantime, *I'll* fool with the boards. Maybe I'll wake somebody else who'll be willing to help. Maybe even one of the crew. Or maybe I'll make a mistake and blow everything up – if you weren't putting me on about that. Think about *that* for a while. Co-operate, or blooey! How about that?'

'I'll think about it,' she said. But she went right on walking.

135

Carl bit his tongue savagely and turned back to the main boards. These goddam do-gooders. In the pinch, they were all alike. Give them a chance to *do* something and they chicken out.

Now it was up to him. It would be nice to know where to find Lavelle. But it was nicer to be sure that Jeanette had him dead wrong. He had a mission now and was above that stuff, at least for the time being. Once he'd reduced the world, he could do better than either of them. Mmmmm.

Raging with hunger, he scraped his fingernails at the powerful little lights.

VI

But he had at last to admit that much of his threat had been simple bravado. The instruments and controls on the board were in obviously related groups, but without technical training he could not even figure out the general categories; and though everything was labelled, the very script the labels were written in was as unbreakable to him as an oscilloscope trace (which it strongly resembled).

Besides, his thinking was obviously not being improved by his having been without a meal for more than a whole day. He decided that he had better be reasonable. The only other course was to wake some crew member, on the chance that a random choice would net him a slave rather than an officer, and try to force him to read the inscriptions; but the risks in that were obvious and frightening. Unless he really wanted to blow up the joint – which in fact he had no intention of chancing – he had to make another try with Jeanette.

She didn't look nearly as haggard as he had hoped, but after all she had both eaten and slept a good deal more recently than he had. Realizing at the same time that he was not only haggard, but untrimmed and dirty, he made an extra effort to be plausible.

'Look, I'm sorry I frightened you. I'm tired, I'm hungry, and I'm on edge. Let's try to talk it all over again sensibly, like civilized people.'

'I don't talk to jailers,' she said coldly.

'I don't blame you. On the other hand, as long as you're bucking me, I have to keep some sort of control over you. You're the only prisoner who knows as much as I know. Hell, you know *more* than I know about some things.'

'The last I heard, you weren't just going to keep me locked up. You were going to torture me.'

136

'What? I said no such –'

'No sleep, no food – what do you call it? Punishment? Persuasion? I know what I call it.'

'All right,' he said. 'I was wrong about that. Why don't we start there? You tell me how to turn the food deliveries back on, and I'll do it. There's no harm in that. We'd both benefit.'

'That's right, you're hungry too. Well, it's controlled by that knob on the side of the sleep-board, as I told you. I'm not sure, but I think it's the third setting on the left – counter-clockwise, that is.'

'Good. I'll see to it that you get fed, and then maybe we can yak again.'

'Maybe.'

At the door, he turned back suddenly. 'This had better not be a gag. If that third setting wakes everybody up or something like that –'

'I don't guarantee a thing,' Jeanette said calmly. 'It's only my best guess. But I don't want the slavers awake again any more than you do. You're no picnic, but I like them even less.'

The point was all the more penetrating for its bluntness. Back in the control room, he set the dial as per instructions, and then raced back to his own cage to try it out. The ship promptly delivered the meal he ordered, and he stuffed himself gorgeously. As an afterthought, he ordered and got a bottle of brandy. He was still determined to puzzle out the control boards as far as possible by himself, and in his present stage of exhaustion a little lubricant might make all the difference.

He knocked on Jeanette's door in passing, but there was no answer.

'Jeanette!' he shouted. 'Jeanette, the food's on!'

Still no response. He wondered if the metal door would pass sound. Then, very faintly, he heard something like a whimper. After a long pause there was another.

He went on, satisfied. He was a little surprised to find that she was able to cry – up to now she had seemed as hard as nails except in her sleep – but it would probably do her good. Besides, it was satisfying to know that she had a breaking point; it would make his persuasions all the more effective, in the long run. And in the meantime, she had heard him announce that there was food available, so she should have a little better opinion of his good faith.

137

He went on up the corridor, cheerfully whistling *Fallout Blues* in two keys at once.

The control room window showed deep night, and had for a long time, when he decided to call himself defeated – temporarily, of course. The brandy had calmed some of his jumpiness and done wonders for his self-confidence, but it hadn't brought into his head any technical knowledge or any safe inspirations, either. And suddenly he was reelingly sleepy. The headache was worse, too.

There should be no danger in catching a little sack time. Everybody was already out except Jeanette, and she was locked in. Of course, she was a sharp apple, and might figure some way of getting out. It would be better to crump her. She'd probably appreciate it, too. It would give him two plusses to start the next conversation with.

He pressed the button that controlled her, and then, avoiding the strip-tease chairs, rolled himself comfortably under the big board.

He awoke slowly and naturally; he had almost forgotten how it felt, after the popped-out-of-nothingness effect that the ships' imposed awakenings produced, and for a little while he simply luxuriated in it. After all, there was no danger. The ship was his.

But it was unusually noisy this morning; a distant snarling of engines, an occasional even more distant murmer of voices –

Voices! He shot upright in alarm.

He was no longer aboard the ship.

Around him was the sunlit interior of a small room, unmistakably barracks-like, with a barred window, furnished only by the narrow single bed in which he had been lying. He himself was clad in grey military-hospital pyjamas, and touching his face, he found that he was clean-shaven – his beard was gone – and had been given a GI haircut. A standard maroon military-hospital robe was folded neatly over the foot of the bed.

An aircraft engine thrummed again outside. Swearing, he ran to the window.

He was indeed locked up beside a military airfield – which one, he had no way of telling, but at least it was American. It was also huge. There was a lot of traffic.

And there was the alien spaceship, right in front of him, grounded. It was probably as much as three miles away, but it was still so enormous as to cut off most of the horizon.

It had been captured – and Carl Wade with it.

He wasted no time wondering how it had been done, or lamenting the collapse of his fantasies, in which, he realized, he had never really believed. The only essential thing now was – *get away*!

He spun to the door, and finding it locked, rattled it furiously.

'Hey!' he shouted furiously. 'Let me out of here! You've got no right – I'm a civilian – and a citizen –'

The lock clicked under his hand, and as he jumped back, there was the sound of a bolt being shot. The door opened and Jeanette came in, followed by two large, impassive, alert Air Force policemen. The girl looked fresh and beautiful; but she too had had a close haircut, all on one side; and there was a massive surgical compress taped under that ear.

'Good morning,' she said.

He continued to back away until he found himself sitting on the bed.

'I might have guessed,' he said. 'So you got the upper hand and sold out.'

'Sold out?' she said, her eyes flashing. 'I had nothing to sell. I couldn't use the ship properly. I turned it over to people who could. My own people – who else?'

'All right, then you chickened out,' Carl said. 'It's the same thing. What are you going to do with me?'

'They tell me you'll be questioned and let go. In your circles, nobody'd be likely to believe anything you say. Just in case any reporter looks you up, the Pentagon's arranged an interview with *Time*. They'll treat your remarks as science-fiction and that'll be the end of you as any sort of witness.'

'And that's all?' he said, amazed.

'That's enough. You're not accused of any crime. Of course, I suspect you committed one against me – but considering that it didn't even wake me up, it can't have been very much more than a token; just kid's stuff.'

This blow to his pride was almost more than he could take, but he was not going to try to set her straight with those two huge flics standing there. He said dully:

'How did you do it?'

'I figured out how the metal people induced sleep in us without our having to wear metal suits. When they first took us on board, they installed a little broadcaster of the sleep-waves, surgically, right next to our skulls – under the right mastoid process. That was what the headache was.'

139

Carl caressed his neck automatically. The headache was gone all that was left was a neat and painless scar.

'But what did you do?'

'I took it out, with your help. When you turned the food service back on, I ordered a tough steak, and I got a sharp knife along with it. Awake, the metal people probably wouldn't have allowed that, but the computers are brainless. So I cut the gadget out. As soon as I got the bleeding stopped, I went forward, found you asleep under the control board, and pressed *your* button. The rest was simple.'

He remembered the faint whimpers he had heard when he had passed the door that night. And he had thought she was softening up!

The worst of it was, in the like circumstances he could never have done it. He was afraid of blood, especially his own.

'Jeanette . . . *Why* did you do it?'

She was silent a long time. At last she said:

'Do you believe in God?'

'Of course not?' he said indignantly. 'Do you?'

'I don't know whether I do or not. But there's one thing I was sure of, right from the start: You'd be a damn poor substitute.'

Harry Harrison

THE GODS THEMSELVES THROW INCENSE

One instant the space ship *Yuri Gagarin* was a thousand-foot long projectile of gleaming metal, the next it was a core of flame and expanding gas, torn fragments and burning particles. Seventy-three people died at that moment painlessly and suddenly. The cause of the explosion will never be determined since all the witnesses were killed and the pieces of wreckage that might have borne evidence were hurtling away from each other towards the corners of infinity. If there had been any outside witness, there in space, he would have seen the gas cloud grow and disperse while the pieces of twisted metal, charred bodies, burst luggage and crushed machines moved out and away from each other. Each had been given its own velocity and direction by the explosion and, though some fragments travelled parallel course for a time, individual differences in speed and direction eventually showed their effect until most fragments of the spatial debris rushed on alone through the immensity of space. Some of the larger pieces had companions: a book of radio-frequency codes orbited the ragged bulk of the ship's reactor, held in position by the gravitic attraction of its mass, while the gape-mouthed, wide eyed corpse of an assistant purser clutched the soft folds of ι woman's dress in its frozen hands. But the unshielded sun scorched the fibres of the cloth while the utter dryness of space desiccated it, until it powdered and tore and centrifugal force pushed it away slowly. It was obviously impossible for anyone to have survived the explosion, but the blind workings of chance that kill may save as well.

There were three people in the emergency capsule and one, the woman, was still unconscious, having struck her head when the ship erupted. One of the two men was in a state of shock, his limbs hanging limply while his thoughts went round and round incessantly like a toy train on a circular track. The other man was tearing at the seal of a plastic flask of vodka.

'All the American ships carry brandy,' he said as he stripped off a curl of plastic then picked at the cap with his nails. 'British ships stock whisky in their medical kits, which is the best idea, but I had to pull this tour on a Russian ship. So look what we get . . .' His words were cut off as he raised the flask to his mouth and drank deeply.

'Thirty thousand pounds in notes,' Damian Brayshaw said thickly. 'Thirty thousand pounds . . . good God . . . they can't hold me responsible.' One heel drummed sluggishly against the padded side of the capsule and moved him away from it a few inches. He drifted slowly back. Even though his features were flaccid with shock, and his white skin even paler now, with a waxen hue, it could be seen that he was a handsome man. His hair, black and cut long, had burst free of its careful dressing and hung in lank strands down his forehead and in front of his eyes. He raised his hands to brush at it, but never completed the motion.

'You want a drink, chum?' the other man asked, holding out the flask. 'I think you need it, chum, knock it back.'

'Brayshaw . . . Damian Brayshaw,' he said, as he took the bottle. He coughed over a mouthful of the raw spirit and for the first time his attention wandered from the lost money, and he noticed the other's dark green uniform with the gold tabs on the shoulders. 'You're a spaceman . . . a ship's officer.'

'Correct. You've got great eyesight. I'm Second Lieutenant Cohen. You can call me Chuck. I'll call you Damian.'

'Lieutenant Cohen, can you tell . . .'

'Chuck.'

'. . . can you tell me what happened. I'm a bit confused.' His actions matched his words as his eyes roamed over the curved padded wall of the closed deadlight, to the wire-cased bulb then back down to the row of handles labelled with incomprehensible Cyrillic characters.

'The ship blew up,' Lieutenant Cohen said tonelessly, but his quick pull at the flask belied the casualness of his words. Years of service in space had carved the deep wrinkles at the corners of his eyes and greyed the barely-seen stubble of his shaven head, yet no

142

amount of service could have prepared him to accept casually the loss of his ship. 'Have some more of this' he said, passing over the vodka flask. 'We have to finish it. Blew up, that's all I knew, just blew up. I had the lock of this capsule open, inspectioncheck, I got knocked halfway through it. You were going by, so I grabbed you and pushed you in, don't you remember?'

Damian hesitated in slow thought, then shook his head *no*.

'Well, I did. Grabbed you, then the girl, she was lying on the deck out cold. Just as I stuffed her in I heard the bulkhead blowing behind me so I climbed in right on top of her. Vacuum sucked the inner hatch shut before I could touch it.'

'The others . . . ?'

'Dead, Damian boy, every single one. Sole survivors, that's us.' Damian gasped. 'You can't be sure,' he said.

'I'm sure. I watched from the port. Torn to pieces. Blew up. The blast sealed off the chunk of ship we were in just long enough for us to get into this can. Even then there wouldn't have been enough time if I hadn't had the lid open and knew the drill. Don't expect those kind of odds to pay off twice in a lifetime.'

'Will anyone find us?' There was a faint tremor in his voice. Chuck shrugged.

'No telling. Give me back the booze before you squeeze the bottle out of shape.'

'You can send a message, there must be a radio in this thing.'

Chick gasped happily after a throat-destroying drink and held the almost empty flask up to the light. 'Save a little to bring the girl around. You must have been out on your feet, Damian lad, you lay right there all the time watching me send the SOS. I stopped just as soon as I tried the receiver.'

'I don't remember. It must have been the shock – but why did you stop transmitting, I don't understand.'

Chuck bent and pulled at one of the handles below them. The padded lid lifted to reveal the controls of a compact transceiver. He flipped a switch and a waterfall-like roar filled the tiny space, then was silenced as he turned it off and closed the lid. Damian shook his head.

'What does that mean?' he asked.

'Solar flare. Storm on the sun. We can never push a signal through that kind of interference. All we can do is hold our water until it stops. Say, it looks like our girl-friend is coming around.'

They both turned to look at her where she lay on the padded wall of the capsule, Damian's eyes widening as he realized for the first time just how attractive she was. Her hair was deep, flaming red, lovely even in the tangled disarray that framed her face. Only the ugly bruise on her forehead marred the pink smoothness of her skin, and her figure was lush, clearly defined by the tight-bodiced, full-skirted dress. The skirt had ridden up, almost to her waist, revealing graceful and supple legs and black lace sequined undergarments.

'Really,' Damian said, putting his hand out, then pulling it back. 'It's not right, shouldn't we . . . adjust her garments?'

'Help yourself,' Chuck smiled. 'But I was enjoying it. I've never seen . . . what do you call them? knickers – quite like that before. Very fancy.' But he was pulling her skirt down even as he said it. Her head turned and she moaned.

'Can she be badly hurt?' Damian asked. 'Have you done anything for her?'

'I have no idea, and no, in that order. Unless you're a doctor. . .'

'No, I'm not.'

'. . . there is nothing we can do. So I let her sleep. When she comes to I'll give her a slug of this paint remover. Never give drink to anyone unconscious, it could get in the lungs, First Aid Course 3B, Space Academy.'

Both men watched, silently, as her eyelids slowly opened, disclosing grey, lovely eyes that moved their gaze across their faces and about the cramped interior of the capsule. Then she began to scream, emptying her lungs in a single spasm of sound then gasping them full again only to repeat the terrified sound. Chuck let her do this three times before he cracked her across the face with his open hand leaving an instant red imprint on the fairness of her skin. The screams broke off and she began to sob.

'You shouldn't . . .' Damian began.

'Of course I should,' Chuck said. 'Medicinal. She got it out of her system and now she's having a good cry. I'm Chuck,' he told the girl, 'and this is Damian. What's your name?'

'What happened to us? Where are we?'

'Chuck and Damian. What's yours?'

'Please tell me. I'm Helena Tyblewski. What happened?'

'I know you, at least I've heard of you.' Damian said. 'You're with the Polish artists at Mooncentre . . .'

'Socialities later, boy. We're in an emergency capsule, Helena, in good shape. We have water, food, oxygen – and a radio to call for help. I'm telling you so you'll realize how well off we are

144

compared with the others aboard the *Yuri*. There was an accident. Everyone else is dead.'

'And ... what will happen to us?'

'A good question. You can help me find out. Drain this vodka bottle, I need the empty flask. And let me have your shoes, yours too, Damian.'

'What are you talking about? What for?'

Chuck began to loosen the wing nuts that held the deadlight sealed in place. 'A fair question,' he said. 'Since I'm the only member of the ship's company present, I'm automatically in command. But we're a little too cramped here for me to pull rank, so I'll tell you what I know and what I want to do. When the accident happened we were, roughly, a quarter of the way from the moon to Earth. Where we are now I have no idea, and it is important to find out.'

The deadlight came free and he swung it to one side, disclosing the capsule's single porthole. Outside, the stars cut ribbons of white light across the darkness, while the Earth made a wider, greenish band.

'As you can see we are rotating about the major axis of this thermos bottle. I'll need star sights to plot our position, which means we have to slow down or stop this thing. Luckily the outer hatch opening faces the direction of motion so anything ejected from it will slow us down. The more the mass and the greater the speed of ejection, the more retardation we'll get. There isn't much surplus to throw away in one of these capsules, that's why I want your shoes. The temperature controls work fine so you won't need them. Okay?'

There were no arguments. Their shoes went into the lock along with the empty flask, some of the padding from the wall, and all the other small items that could be accumulated. Chuck sealed the inner hatch and pumped in oxygen from the tanks to raise the pressure as high as possible. When he threw the handle that opened the hatch on the outer door, the capsule seemed to start spinning around them and they tumbled together against the wall.

'Sorry,' Damian said, reddening as he realized that his arms were around Helen and he was lying on top of her. She smiled as they drifted away from the padding and there was suddenly no up and down as they floated in free fall. Chuck frowned at the stars moving leisurely by the port.

'That should be good enough to get some sightings. If not we can jettison some more junk.'

145

He unclipped his comparison dectant from the holder on his belt and pointed it out the port, squinting through it. 'That is going to take awhile,' he said, 'so relax. With this gadget I can measure the angular distance of up to five astronomical objects, it will remember the angles and its tiny, microminiaturized brain can even do some of the basic computations. But it will take time. So let's trade confidences, get to know each other, real chummy if you get what I mean. Me, I'm the simple one. Bronx High School, Columbia, the Academy – then the moon run ever since. What about you, Helena? Our limey friend said you were an artiste. A singer? Going to let us have an aria or two?'

Helena compressed her lips. 'I am not *that* sort of artiste. I create, the newest and most expressive art form, light mobiles.'

'I've seen them,' Chuck said, sighting on another star. 'They always hurt my eyes and give me a headache. What about you, Damian, are you a bank robber or an embezzler?'

'Sir!'

'Well don't blame me for asking, not after all that mumbling you were doing about thirty thousand pounds, gone, gone.'

Damian clutched his hands together, tightly. 'I'm with the British Embassy. It was currency, in my charge. I was transferring it back to Earth. Now it's gone . . .'

Chuck laughed. 'Don't be an idiot. It's just paper, it's been destroyed. They'll just write it off and print some more.'

Damian smiled sheepishly. 'You're right, of course. I never stopped to think of that after the accident. Stupid of me.'

'We all have our bad days. Now talk to yourselves for a couple of minutes while I run these figures through the meatgrinder.'

The conversation lagged while he pecked at the tiny computer and, as the first shock of the tragedy faded the other two began to feel the pressing loneliness of their position. Once they stopped talking the only sound was the almost inaudible hum of the air-circulating fan, and the occasional click of the computer. The naked bulb shone down, the stars drifted by in the blackness of the port. They were warm and comfortable in their capsule. Six feet by twelve feet inside. A container of comfort, one man wide and two men high, packed with the necessities to sustain life. Yet two inches away, on the other side of the insulated wall, was the endless emptiness of space.

'That's that,' Chuck said, and slipped the dectant back into its sheath. 'Now let's see what the chow is like in this commy canister.' The others almost smiled at the welcome hoarseness of his voice.

'What about your figures? Where are we?' Helena asked.

'I have no idea,' Chuck said, throwing back a large padded lid in the end of the capsule. 'That's not exactly correct. I have a reading that places us somewhere between the Earth and the moon. But I wasn't on the bridge and I have no idea where we were before the explosion. So I'll wait awhile, at least an hour, then I'll shoot some more sights. Comparing the two positions should give us an idea of our course and speed. Anyone thirsty?' He reached in and removed one of the containers of water that were ranked like giant bullets in a clip.

'I will take some, please,' Helena said.

'Just suck it through the teat in the end. . .'

'I have drunk it free fall before, thank you.'

'Sorry, sweetheart, I forgot you were an old space hand. Something to eat with it?' He withdrew a flat, brownish package and frowned at it. 'Looks like a cardboard deck of cards. Can anyone here read Russian better than I can.'

'I'm sure I can,' Helena said, taking the package and glancing at it briefly. 'These are *latkes*, it says so clearly on the outside.'

'Dehydrated potato pancakes . . .' he choked out. 'I'm beginning to think the rest of the people in the *Yuri* were the lucky ones.'

'Not even in jest,' Damian said. 'Touch wood when you say that.'

'I doubt if there is any in this capsule, if you don't count the *latkes*.'

When they had finished, Chuck counted the stores, then opened another lid to check the reading on the meter attached to the oxygen tanks. He tried the radio again, but there was only the waterfall of static. At the end of an hour he did his observations once more, then computations.

'Well, I'll be damned,' he said.

'Is something wrong?' Damian asked.

'Let me check again.'

Only after he had done everything a third time did he speak to them. There was no humour in his voice now.

'I'll lay it right on the line. We're in trouble. We had the luck to be behind the explosion – in relation to the ship's direction of travel, that is – and it had the effect of cancelling a good part of our momentum.'

'I don't understand what you are talking about,' Helena said firmly.

'Then I'll simplify it. If the ship hadn't blown it would have reached earth in about two days. But this capsule doesn't have the same speed anymore. It's going to be three to four weeks before we get near enough to Earth to send a message and be picked up.'

'So what is wrong with that? It will be uncomfortable certainly, the lack of privacy here with you two men...'

'Will you let me finish. It will be more than uncomfortable, it will be deadly. We have food – though we could go without eating for that long – the water is recycled so there is no shortage there. But these capsules are too small to carry CO_2 regenerators. Our oxygen will run out in about two weeks. We'll be a week dead before we can send a message that anyone can hear and act on.'

'Is there no way out?' Damian asked.

'I don't know. If we...'

'This is nonsense!' Helena burst in. 'We can radio the moon, Earth, they'll send ships.'

'It's not that easy,' Chuck said. 'I know what ships there are on the moon and I know their range. We're practically outside their zone of operation now, not forgetting the fact that we can't even contact them. If the solar storm lasts even a few hours more we have to write them off. They won't even be able to pick up our signals by that time. After that it is the long haul to Earth, contacting one of the satellite stations, waiting while they plot our position and a ship can reach us. Three weeks absolute minimum, probably four.'

Helena began to cry then, and he didn't try to stop her. It was something to cry about. He waited until she had finished and then, since neither of the others had seemed to see the obvious answer, he told them, in a flat and toneless voice.

'The amount of air that three people breathe in two weeks is the same amount that two people breathe in three weeks. It might even last a little longer with proper care.'

There was a long moment of silence before Damian spoke.

'You do realize what you are saying? There is no other way out of this?'

'I've gone over everything, every possibility. This is the only way that some of us stand a chance. Sure death for three. A

148

fifty-fifty chance for two. Not good odds, but better than no odds.'

'But – someone will have to die to give the others a chance to live?'

'Yes, putting it simply, that's that way it will have to be.'

Damian took a deep breath. 'And the one to die won't be you. You're needed to navigate and to work the radio – '

'Not at all. Though I confess to a sneaking wish that it really were that way. The navigation is done. It will take me about ten minutes to show you both how to operate the radio and call for help. There is unlimited power from the solar cells so the signal can go out continuously once the solar storm is over.'

'That is – well – very decent of you. You could have told us differently and we would have believed you. Makes it a bit easier on me, if you know what I mean. For a moment there, with Miss Tyblewski out of it, it looked like I was going to be the reluctant volunteer. So it is you or I. . .'

'No, one of the three of us,' Chuck said.

'I'm sorry, you can't possibly mean that a woman . . .'

'I can and do. This is no game, Damian, of women and children first into the lifeboat. This is death, one hundred per cent certain that I am talking about. All lives are equal. We are all in this together. I'm sure Helena appreciates your gesture, but I don't think she is the kind of person who wants to take advantage of it. Am I right?' he asked, turning to the girl.

'You're a pig,' she hissed. 'A fat, stupid pig.'

'I'm wrong,' Chuck said flatly, facing Damian. 'I'll issue the order and take the responsibility. You can both sign it as witnesses, under protest if you like . . .'

'You want to kill me, I know, to save yourself,' Helena shouted. 'You don't care. . .'

'Please, don't,' Damian said, taking her by the arms, but she shook him off, pushing him so hard he hit the opposite side of the capsule.

'. . . who do you think you are to set yourself up as a judge of life and death!'

'I am the officer in charge of this vessel,' Chuck said in a voice of great weariness. 'There are rules and orders for this sort of occasion and I am on my oath to follow them. This is the correct procedure, and equal chance for all to survive, no favouritism.'

'You are just using that for an excuse.'

'You are welcome to think so. However, I agree with the rule and think it the only just one. . .'

'I'll have nothing to do with it.'

'That is your choice. But the results are binding on you whether you partake or not.' He looked over at Damian who, white-faced, had been listening silently. 'You talk to her, Damian, perhaps she'll listen to you. Or do you agree with her?'

'I . . . really don't know. It is so hard to say. But we, that is there isn't much choice, really.'

'None,' Chuck said.

It was something Damian would never have considered doing before, putting his arms about a girl whom he had just met, but everything was very different now. He held her and she leaned against him and sobbed and it was very natural for both of them.

'Let's get this over with,' Chuck said, 'the worst thing we can do is wait. And we'd all better agree beforehand what is going to happen. I have three identical squares of plastic here, and I've marked one of them with an X. Take a look at them. And three pieces of brown wrapper from this food packet. You do it, Damian, twist a piece of wrapper around each square, twist each one the same way so they can't be told apart. Now shake them up in your cupped hands so you don't know which is which. All right. Let them float right there in the middle where we can all see them.'

Damian opened his cupped hands and the three twists of plastic drifted in free fall. One floated away from the others and he prodded it back into position. They all stared, they could not help themselves, fixedly and intently at the tiny scraps of destiny.

'Here's what will happen next,' Chuck said. 'We'll each take one. I'll draw last. I have a pill in my belt, it's standard spacer gear, and whoever draws the piece with the X takes the pill six hours from now –' He looked at his watch. '– at exactly 1900 hours. Is it understood and agreed? This is it. There is no going back or mind-changing later. Now and forever. Agreed?'

Tight-lipped, Damian only gave a quick nod. Helena said or did nothing beyond flashing Chuck a look of utter hatred.

'It is agreed then,' he said. 'The pill is instantaneous and absolutely painless. Here we go. Helena, do you want to draw first?'

'No,' she said unbelievingly. 'You can't . . .'

'We have no other choice, do we,' Damian told her, and managed to smile. 'Here, let me draw first. You can have the second one.'

'Don't open it,' Chuck said as Damian reached out and took the nearest one. 'Go ahead, Helena, none of us is enjoying this.'

She did not move until Chuck shrugged and reached for a wrapper marker himself. Then her hand lashed out and she clutched the one he had been about to take. 'That's mine,' she said.

'Whatever you say,' Chuck smiled wryly and took the remaining one. 'Open them up,' he said.

The others did not move, so he carefully unwrapped his and held up the square. It was blank on both sides. Helena gasped.

'Well, I'm next I imagine,' Damian said and slowly unfolded his. He looked at it, then quickly closed his fist.

'We have to see it too,' Chuck told him.

Damian slowly opened his hand to show a blank.

'I knew it would be a trick!' Helena screamed and threw hers from her. Damian caught it when it rebounded from the wall, opened it at arm's length to reveal the scrawled, black X.

'I'm sorry,' he whispered, not looking at her.

'I think we need a drink,' Chuck told them as he twisted about to burrow in one of the lockers. 'There are at least four more litres of vodka stowed down here with the water jugs, for some obscure Russian reason, and now is the time we can use them.'

Damian took a deep breath so his voice wouldn't shake when he talked. 'I'm sorry, I can't go along with this. If we come out of this I couldn't live with myself. I think I had better take Helena's place. . .'

'No!' Chuck Cohen said, outwardly angry for the first time. 'It invalidates everything, all the choosing. You've put your life on the line – isn't that enough? Death hits by chance in space, the way it hit the others on the ship and missed us. It has hit again. The matter is closed.' He pulled out a container and started by drinking a good fifth of it in one gulp.

Perhaps that was why the vodka was there. Helena, still unbelieving, drank because it was handed to her by the two men who could not look her in the eye. It numbed. If you drank enough it numbed.

The stars slipped by outside the uncovered port, the thermostat kept the temperature at a comfortable 22 degrees centigrade and the fan hummed as it circulated the air, pumping in metered amounts of the oxygen, each minute lowering the infinitely precious level in the tanks.

'Lower metabolism . . .' Chuck said, then closed his eyes so he wouldn't see the spinning walls of the capsule – now the two others who were at the end of the capsule, as far as they could get from him. He found his mouth with the flask and sucked in a burning measure of the liquid. 'Metabolism is oxidation and we gotta save oxygen. Don't eat, eat less, burn less. Go three weeks without food. Good for the figure. Lie down. Move less, burn less . . . oxygen. . .' His grumbling voice died away and the plastic flask floated free of his limp fingers.

'No, no, I can't,' Helena sobbed and held to Damian. She had drunk little, but fear had affected her even more strongly.

'No, you shouldn't, shouldn't,' Damian said and drank again because he did not know what to do. He bent to kiss her hair and somehow had his lips against the tear-cold dampness of her cheek then on the full warmth of her mouth.

She was suddenly aware of him. Her lips responded and her arms were about him, her body pressing against him, her legs thrusting. They floated freely in the air, rotating slowly locked in tight embrace.

'I want you, I don't want to die, I can't, I can't,' Helena sobbed and took his hand, putting it inside her dress on to the bare, warm, firmness of her breast. 'Help me, help me. . .'

Damian kissed her in a roaring wave of sensation. He knew that the spaceman was there, unconscious, only feet away, yet he didn't care. The escape from the wreck, the unbearable tension of gambling with his own life, the amount he had drunk, the closeness of death, the passion of the woman's flesh against his, all of this combined to wipe away everything except the burning awareness of her presence and the rising passion she evoked.

'Come to me, I need you,' she whispered in his ear, then took it hard between her teeth. 'I can't die. Why should I? He wants it, that pig. Only he wants it. He wants death, why can't he die? Why didn't he leave me in the ship? He gave me my life and now he will take it away again. And you too, you'll see, after me he'll find a way to kill you. What does he need either of us for? You can't believe a thing he said, why should we? He's brutal, deadly, a monster. He's going to kill me. You want me and he is going to kill me.'

'Helena . . .' he whispered, as his flesh touched hers.

'No!' she wailed and pushed him from her. He did not under-

152

stand, he pressed forward again but she held him from her. 'No, I cannot, I want to, but I cannot. Not with him here, not before I die. But I do want you. . .'

Then she was gone, and when he turned to look for her he became dizzy and saw her bending over the end of the capsule. Time moved strangely, too fast, yet slow at the same time. She was gone a long time, yet she was suddenly back and putting something cold into his hand.

'Take this,' she whispered, 'it's from the medical kit. I can't do it, you must. Someone must die. He must die, you can do it. He is the biggest. Do it then come back to me. I'll be here, I'll be with you always, just do this for me.'

Blinking, Damian looked down at the glittering scalpel on his palm, at her hand closing his fingers over it. 'Do it!' she breathed and pulled him, drifting, the length of the tiny space until he hung over the snoring spaceman. 'DO IT!' the voice said and, not knowing quite what he was doing or why, he raised his fist high.

'There!' her voice said and her finger swam before him touching the sleeping man on the side of the neck, just on a thick and pulsing artery.

'Do it!' her lips touched moistly down his face and in a sudden spasm he struck down at the bare flesh.

It was the bellow of a wounded beast. Sober, awake in the instant, with the pain tearing red fingers into his neck. Chuck reared up, lashing out with his hands. The scalpel was plunged an inch deep into his flesh, lodging in the thick mastoid muscle of his neck, bleeding floating red spheres into the air.

His hands clutched Damian and, still roaring with agony, he began to beat him as only a spacer knows how to do, holding one hand behind his head so he could not recoil away while the other fist pounded and crushed his face. Damian fought back, trying to escape the pain, but there was no escape. As they battled Helena's voice shattered about them.

'He tried to kill you, Chuck, he wanted me but I told him no. So he tried to kill you while you slept. A coward! Rape me, he tried . . . kill him . . . put him out of the ship. Here, the port!'

She pushed over to the airlock and opened the inner port as she had seen him do earlier. The lock was just big enough for a man. 'In here!' she screeched.

Her words came through Chuck's anger and fitted it, telling

153

him what he really wanted to do. Holding the other by the throat he spun him across the capsule and began to jamb him, struggling, into the tiny space. The scalpel fell from his neck and slowly droplets bubbled in its wake.

Damian's body went suddenly limp and Chuck pushed in the legs and then a dangling arm.

'No, you don't have to force me,' Damian said quietly. 'It's all right now. I'll go. I deserve it.'

Something of the man's tones penetrated Chuck's rage and he hesitated, blinking at the other.

'It's only fair,' Damian said. 'I attacked you, I admit that, tried to kill you. It doesn't matter that she used herself to make me do it, promised everything – then helped you when she saw I hadn't succeeded. There was something in me that let me do it. . .'

'Don't believe him, he's lying!' Helena wailed.

'No, I have no reason to lie. I'm taking your place, Helena, so at least don't vilify me. I tried to kill him for you – and for myself.'

'She wanted you to do this?' Chuck said thickly, blinking through his pain.

'You both want me dead,' she screamed, then tore at the heavy computer on Chuck's belt. He groped for it as she pulled it loose and was only half turned towards her when heavy pain and blackness crushed against his skill.

'About time you came around,' Damian said. 'Drink this.'

Chuck felt the bandage on his neck when he bent to put the spout to his lips. He looked around the room while he sucked in the water. 'How long have I been out?' he asked.

'About nine hours. You lost some blood and you have a hole in your head.'

'There are just two of us here?'

'That's right,' Damian said, and the smile was gone now. 'Maybe I figured this wrong, but it's over and done now. I tried to kill you. I didn't succeed and – fairly enough – you tried to kill me right back. But neither of us managed to finish the job. Maybe I'm thinking wrong, but I feel the score is even now and no recriminations.'

'You don't hear me complaining. And Helena?'

Damian looked uncomfortable. 'Well . . . the six hours were almost up. And she did agree on the drawing. And she did lose. She – attacked me with the scalpel. I'm afraid your computer was completely smashed. I had to dispose of it.'

154

'The insurance will replace it,' Chuck said hoarsely. 'God, my neck hurts. Head, too.'

'Do you think we'll make it?' Damian asked.

'The odds are a hell of a lot better now than they were nine hours ago.'

'Yes, one could say that. Perhaps the powers that be have been propitiated by Miss Tyblewski's noble gesture. *Upon such sacrifices. . . . The gods themselves throw incense*.' He looked out, unseeing at the blackness beyond the port. 'Do you think that should we get out of this, we should, well, mention Helena . . ?'

'Helena who?' Chuck said. 'Seventy-four people died when the *Yuri Gagarin* blew. We're the sole survivors.'

THE GHOUL SQUAD

I

'Look at them,' Patrolman Charlie Vandeem said, jerking his thumb towards the grey vehicle parked on the other side of the road – then spitting in the same direction. 'Just sitting there like vultures waiting for their pound of flesh. Vultures.'

'The ITB have a job to do and they're doing it,' Doc Hoyland said, pushing his fingers up under the back of the girl's jaw to find the fluttering pulse. 'What did the ambulance say, Charlie? How long will they be?'

'Ten minutes more at least. They were way out on the other side of town when the call came in.' He looked down at the girl stretched out on the ground, at the thin limbs and cheap cotton dress, stained now with blood, and the bandage that covered her head like a turban. She was young, almost pretty: he turned quickly away and the grey bulk of the ITB wagon was still there waiting.

'The ITB!' the young patrolman said loudly, 'you know what people call them, Doc?'

'The Isoplastic Transplantation Bank . . .'

'No, you know what I mean. They call them the Ghoul Squad, and you know why.'

'I know why, and I also know that is no way for a law officer to talk. They've got an important job to do.' His voice changed as he pressed tighter, groping for the vanishing flutter of the pulse, weaker than a dying butterfly's wing. 'She's not going to make it, Charlie, ambulance or no. She didn't bleed much but . . . half her brain is gone.'

'There must be something you can do.'

'Sorry Charlie, not this time.' He pulled the loose collar of her dress down and felt the back of her neck. 'Make a note for the record that she is not wearing a necklace and that there is no medallion.'

'Are you sure?' the patrolman asked, flapping open his notebook. 'Maybe it fell and broke down her dress . . .'

'Maybe it didn't. The chains are made of metal. Do *you* want to look?'

Although he was in his thirties Charlie was still young enough to blush. 'Now don't go getting teed off at me, Doc, that was just for the record. We have to be sure.'

'Well I'm sure. Write that down, and the time, and what you see for yourself.' He stood and waved his arm. The grey I T B truck rumbled to life and started over to them.

'What are you doing?'

'She's dead. No pulse, no respirations. Just as dead as the other two.' He nodded towards the still smoking wreck of the pickup truck. 'It just took a few minutes longer. She was really dead when they hit that tree, Charlie, there was never any chance.'

Behind them the heavy tyres braked to a stop and there was a slam as the rear door of the vehicle was thrown open. A man jumped down from the cab: the initials I T B in neat white letters were on the pocket of his grey uniform, the same grey as the truck. He spoke into a hand recorder as he approached.

'Eight April, 1976, on State Highway 34, approximately 17 miles west of Loganport, Georgia. Victim of an auto wreck, female, caucasian, in her early twenties, cause of death . . .' he paused and looked up at Dr Hoyland.

'Massive brain trauma. Almost the entire left frontal lobe of the cerebrum is gone.'

As the driver came around the truck, snapping open a folding stretcher, the first I T B man turned to the patrolman.

'This is now a medical matter, officer,' he said, 'and no longer a police concern. Thanks for your help.'

Charlie had a quick temper. 'Are you trying to get rid of me?'

Doc Hoyland took him by the arm and turned him away.

'The answer is yes. You have no more business here now than you have in, well, in an operating theatre. These men have a job to do, and it must be done quickly.'

Charlie's mind was made up for him as he heard the approaching wail of the ambulance. He went to flag it down and his back was turned as they bent and cut the clothes from the girl's body. Working quickly now they placed the corpse on to the stretcher and drew a sheet of sterile plastic over it. A heavy curtain covered the open rear of the vehicle and they raised the bottom a bit to slide the stretcher under it.

When the patrolman turned back the men were already swinging the doors shut. At his feet was the blanket from the patrol car, speckled with the girl's blood and littered with the crumpled rags that had been her garments. A puff of vapour rose from the top of a vent of the grey vehicle.

'Doc – what are they doing in there?'

The doctor was tired. He had had very little sleep the night before, and his temper was getting short.

'You know just as well as I do what they are doing,' he snapped 'The ITB does a good job and a vital one. Only fools and crackpots think differently.'

Charlie said *ghouls* as he started to the car to radio a report, but he didn't say it loud enough for the doc to hear.

II

This Christmas, in the year 1999, was really one for celebrations. Something about the new century being just a few days away seemed to excite everyone, that and the general prosperity and the tax cut that had been President Greenstein's holiday present to the entire country. What with Christmas falling on a Monday this year and the 26th now being an official holiday as well, the four-day weekend had been a very very merry one. Someone had said that all the corn likker drunk in this one county would have floated a battleship and he was probably right, if it was a small battleship.

Sheriff Charlie Vandeen was nowhere near as tired as his deputies. In fact, he had to admit, he wasn't tired at all. He had not been home since the fire on the night of the 23rd but that didn't mean much. He had a cot in the room behind his office and he slept there, just as comfortably as in his bachelor apartment. His deputies knew where to find him in an emergency and that was good enough most of the time. Anyway, it hadn't been that kind of holiday weekend, nothing really big, just a lot of everything little. Fires, drunks and fender benders, fights and noisy parties. Sheriff Charlie had had a good sleep. Now, showered and shaved

158

and wearing a clean pressed uniform, he looked out at the foggy drab dawn of December 26th and wished the whole blamed holiday was over and people were back to work. The birthday of the Prince of Peace, the reverend had said that in church during the midnight service, when Charlie had looked in, which was his duty but not his pleasure. People sure had funny ideas how to celebrate that kind of birthday. He yawned and sipped at the steaming black coffee. Off in the distance there was a growing rumble: he looked at his watch. The morning hoverliner from the Bahamas, right on time.

Leaning back in the chair he unconsciously slipped into a familiar daydream. Something he always hoped to do. The drive to Macon, to the big hoverterminal on the Ocmulgee river outside of town. His bag whisked away, then up the gangplank into the arena-sized hoverliner. He'd be in the Top-side Bar when they left, he'd seen enough pictures of it to know just what it would be like, looking down at the world rushing by. He'd have a Mint Julep first, to celebrate his leaving, then Jamaica Rum Punch to celebrate the holiday ahead. He would sit up there, king of the castle, getting quietly wiped out while the pine slashes and swamps whooshed by below. Then the beach and the blue ocean and the golden islands ahead, the luxury hotel and the girls. In the daydream he always had a nice bronze tan when he walked out on to the beach, and he was a good bit younger. The grey streaks were gone from his hair and his gut was a good fifteen inches smaller. When the girls looked at him . . .

Through the reverie he was suddenly aware that the distant rumble had stopped. At the same moment the sky, above the low hanging fog, lit up in a sudden rosy glare.

'Oh my God,' he said, standing, unaware that the chair had fallen over backward and that the cup had dropped from his fingers, crashing to the floor. 'Something's happened to it.'

The hovercraft was foolproof, that's what they said, floating safely on a cushion of air, moving over land and water with equal ease. If, for some unaccountable reason, the engines should fail, they were supposed to simply sink down, to float or stand until they could move again. They were supposed to. There still had been some close calls, collisions and the like. When something the size of an ocean liner rushes along at over 150 miles an hour accidents are always possible. It looked like the laws of chance had finally come up with a zero. Luck had run out. He reached for the phone.

While a deputy alerted the cars and the new ambulance service, fire department as well, he verified the fact that a hoverliner, in this area, did not answer their call signal. He reported what he had seen and heard and hung up. He still hoped that his suspicions were wrong, but it was a very slight hope.

Jamming his hat on to his head he kicked in to his high-heeled boots at the same time, then ran for the door grabbing up his raincoat and gunbelt on the way. Unit three was parked at the kerb outside and Ed Homer was dozing over the wheel. He jerked awake when the Sheriff climbed in next to him: he hadn't heard the explosion. As they pulled away Charlie sent out an all units alarm. . . There was no telling what they would find out there. He still hoped that he was wrong, but by now it was a mighty small hope.

'Do you think it hit in the swamp, Sheriff?' Ed asked, flooring the turbine and burning rubber down the highway.

'No, wasn't far enough west from what I could tell. And if it was we couldn't reach it in any case. I think it's still in the Cut.'

'I'll take Johnson's road out, then the farm road along the Cut.'

'Yeah,' Charlie said, buckling on his gun.

It was full daylight now, watery and grey, but they still needed their lights for the patches of fog. They braked and broadsided into the side of the road and Ed touched the siren to pull over a lumbering milktruck on collection rounds. After that it was a straight run to the Cut, the broad highway through the pines that the hovercraft used. Grain couldn't be grown here, the downblast from the air cushion blew the kernels from their stalks, and grazing animals panicked when the big craft passed. A cash crop of grass for fodder was still possible, and the Cut was an immensely long meadow before it ran into the swamp. The cruiser bumped along the dirt track the harvesters used and there, dimly seen through the rising fog, was a boiling column of black smoke.

Ed Homer, wide-eyed, automatically took his foot from the accelerator as they came close. The hoverliner was gigantic in death, cracked open and smoking, tilted up where it had nosed into the trees after dragging an immense raw furrow for 500 yards through the field.

They drove slowly towards it, passing great tumbled sheets of black skirting torn from the bottom of the liner. People were climbing out of the wreck, lying in the grass, helping others to safety. The car braked to a stop and when the turbine died they could hear the cries and shocked moans of pain.

'Get on the network and tell them exactly where we are,' the Sheriff said, throwing open the door. 'Tell them we're going to need all the medical aid they can find. Fast. Then help to get those people clear.'

He ran towards the wrecked liner, to the people sprawled on the ground. Some of them were burned and bloody, some of them obviously dead, some of them uninjured though still numb from the sudden shock. Two men in uniform carried a third: his right leg hung at an impossible angle and there was a belt about his thigh that cut deeply into the flesh. He stifled a moan as they put him down before turning back to the wreck. The Sheriff saw that the man was still conscious, though his skin was parchment white under the bruises and oil smears.

'Is there any chance of more fire or explosion,' he asked the man. At first the officer could only gasp, then gained a measure of control.

'Don't think so . . . automatic extinguishers kicked in when the engines blew. That's under control. But there is sure to be fuel leakage. No smoking, open fires, must tell them . . .'

'I'll see to that. Just take it easy, the ambulances are on the way.'

'People inside . . .'

'We'll get them out.'

The Sheriff started towards the looming wreck, then stopped. The crew and male passengers seemed to be organized now. People were being helped to safety, even carried out on stretchers. It was more important for him to wait here for the assistance that would be arriving soon. He went back to the car and flicked the microphone switch from radio to bullhorn.

'May I have your attention please.' He twisted the volume up full and the heads turned as the amplified voice rolled over them. 'This is the Sheriff speaking. I've called in medical aid and they'll be arriving at any moment now. I have been told that there may be fuel leakage and danger of fire – but there is no fire now. But do not smoke or light matches . . .'

There was a fluttering roar from behind him, growing louder. A copter, a big multirotor one. This would be the ambulance people. Dust rolled out as the machine dropped close by and he put his back to it. When the blades slowed he turned to look. It was grey from nose to tail and Sheriff Charlie Vandeen felt that same hot needle of anger that had not lessened after all the years. He ran towards it as the entrance-way dropped down.

'Get back inside, you're not wanted here,' he called out to the two men who were hurrying down. They stopped, surprised.

'Who are you?' the first man asked. His hair, beneath his cap, was almost the same grey as the rest of his uniform.

'I'm the Sheriff, you can read, can't you?' He tapped at his badge, at the large clear letters, black on gold, but his fingers only brushed against the fabric of his shirt. Surprised, he looked down at the two empty holes in his pocket. When he had put on a clean uniform he hadn't changed his badge from the old one.

'You heard what I said,' he called out to the men who had passed him while his attention had been on the missing badge. 'The Ghoul Squad isn't needed here, not in my county.'

The older man turned and looked back at him coldly.

'So you are that sheriff. I know about your county. Nevertheless we are doctors and since there are no other medical personnel present we intend to function in that capacity.' He looked down at the Sheriff's hand which rested on his pistol butt. 'If you intend to fire upon us for doing that you will have to shoot us in the back.' He turned and both men started walking quickly towards the wreck.

The Sheriff pulled his gun up a bit, then cursed and shoved it back. All right, fine, they were doctors. Let them act like doctors for once. That was okay by him.

Sirens sounded down the cut and there were more copters coming in low over the trees. He saw Ed Homer helping a woman from the wreck and almost went to help, until he realized that he could do far more out here. Every kind of assistance would be arriving now and they would need organizing if they weren't to start falling over each other. The fire department pumper was bouncing across the field and they ought to get right up against the wreck to make sure there would be no fires. He ran out and waved to them.

Bit by bit organization replaced confusion. The unhurt passengers were guided from the area and the medical teams went to work on the wounded. Two local doctors had heard the call on the emergency network and had been temporarily drafted into the teams. One of them was old Doc Hoyland, in his seventies now and semi-retired, who still rushed out like a firehorse when he heard the bell. He was needed today.

There was a growing row of figures covered with blankets that the Sheriff glanced at once, then turned away. When he did this he saw two men in grey carrying a stretcher towards their copter.

In sudden anger he ran towards them, to the base of the entrance-way.

'Is that man dead?' he asked, glancing quickly at the gaping mouth and staring, unmoving eyes. The lead stretcher-bearer looked at the Sheriff and almost smiled.

'Are you kidding? That's the only kind we ever go near. Now get out of the way –'

'Take him and put him over there with the other victims.' Charlie touched the butt of his revolver, then grabbed it firmly. 'That is an order.'

The men hesitated, not knowing what to do, until the rear bearer said, 'Set,' and they put the stretcher on the ground. He thumbed his pocket radio to life and talked quickly into it.

'Over there,' the Sheriff said, pointing. 'I mean it and I'm playing no games.' The men bent reluctantly just as the ITB doctor, whom the Sheriff had first talked to came hurrying up. There were two State Troopers with him, both of whom the Sheriff knew by sight. The Sheriff spoke even as the doctor opened his mouth.

'You better load your ITB ghouls back aboard, doc, and get out of here. There's going to be no hunting on my game preserve.'

The doctor shook his head, almost sadly. 'No, it is not going to be that way at all. I told you that we knew about you, Sheriff, and that we have been avoiding trouble by keeping our units from entering your area of jurisdiction. We do not wish any public differences of opinion. However, this time we have no recourse but to make our position clear. The ITB is a federal agency established by federal law and no local authorities may interfere with it. We cannot create a precedent here. Therefore I must ask you to stand aside so that these men may pass.'

'No!' the Sheriff said hoarsely, colour flooding his cheeks. 'Not in my county . . .' He stepped back, his hand still on his gun as the two State Troopers approached. The first one nodded at him.

'What the doctor says is right, Sheriff Vandeen. The law is on his side. Now you don't want to cause yourself any trouble.'

'Step back!' the Sheriff shouted, pulling at his gun, a loud roaring in his ears. Before it slid clear of the holster the two troopers were there, one on each side, holding him firmly. He struggled against them, gasping in air, trying to ignore the growing pain in his chest. Then he slumped forward suddenly, a dead weight.

The ITB doctor had the Sheriff flat on the ground and was bent over him when Dr Hoyland hurried up.

'What happened?' he asked, slipping his stethoscope from his pocket. He tore open the Sheriff's shirt and put the pickup against his chest while he listened to the explanation. He opened his bag and gave the prone man a swift injection.

'Just what you might have expected,' he said, struggling to stand. A trooper helped him to his feet. His face was as wrinkled as a hound dog's and had the same solemn expression. 'But you can't talk to Charlie Vandeen. Angina pectoris, he's had it for years. Progressive heart deterioration. He's supposed to take it easy, you see how well he listens to me.' A fine rain, no heavier than mist, was beginning to fall. The doctor drew his chin down inside his coat collar like an ancient turtle. 'Get him out of this,' he ordered.

The ITB men put the corpse aside and gently placed the Sheriff on to the stretcher. They carried it into their copter and the two doctors followed. Inside the body of the copter there was a narrow corridor formed by the curved inner wall and a partition of thin transparent plastic sheeting that stretched when they pressed against it. The Sheriff was breathing hoarsely, laboriously, and his eyes were open now.

'I have been after him for the last five years to have a heart transplant. The one he's got is not strong enough to pump soda-pop.' Dr Hoyland looked down, frowningly grim, while one of the stretcher bearers covered the Sheriff with a blanket, up to the shoulders.

'He wouldn't do it?' the ITB doctor asked.

'No. Charlie has a thing about transplants and the ITB.'

'I have noticed that,' the doctor said, dryly. 'Do you know why?'

The voices were distant, garbled hums to Charlie Vandeen, but his eyes worked well enough. He saw the two men carrying a stretcher with a man's body on it. They pushed it against the plastic wall which parted like a great obscene mouth and drew it in. It was now in a small room walled with plastic where a man waited, dressed and masked in white. He stripped the body nude in an instant, then sprayed it all over with a nozzle hooked to a tank on the wall. Then, dripping with fluid, the corpse was rolled on to a plastic sheet and pushed through the other wall of this cell into the larger inside room.

Here the ghouls waited. Charlie did not want to look but he

could not stop himself. On the table. A single practised cut opened the body from sternum to pubis. Then dissection began. Something was removed from the gaping wound and, with long tongs, dropped into a container. Fumes rose up. Charlie moaned.

Dr Hoyland nodded. 'Of course I know why Charlie acts this way. It's no secret, it's just that nobody talks about it. He had a shock, right in the family, when he had just joined the state troopers. His kid sister, no more than sixteen as I remember, driving home from a school dance. Bunch of wiseacre kids, a hotrod, some moonshine, a crackup, you know the story.'

The ITB doctor nodded a little sadly. 'Yes I do. And her medallion ... ?'

'She left it home. She was wearing her first party dress, low neck, and it showed.'

Through a thickening haze the Sheriff saw something else, red and dripping, taken from the body and put into the box. He groaned aloud.

'It's going to take more than that shot,' Dr Hoyland said. 'Do you have one of those new portable heart-lung machines here?'

'Yes, of course, I'll get it rigged.' He pointed to his assistant who hurried away. 'I cannot blame him for hating us, but it is all so useless. When the immune response was finally overcome in the seventies there were just no organs and limbs available for the people who desperately needed them. So the Congress passed the ITB law. If people do not want their bodies used to benefit others they simply wear a medallion that states this fact. They will never be touched. The act of not wearing a medallion means that the person involved is ready to donate whatever parts of his body may be needed. It's a fair law.'

Dr Hoyland grunted. 'And a tricky one. People lose medallions or never get round to getting them and so forth.'

'Here comes the machine now. It's a very just law. No one loses by it. Most of the religions – as well as the atheists – agree that the body is just so much inert chemicals after death. If these chemicals can benefit mankind where is the argument? The ITB takes the bodies without medallions and removes the parts that we know are vitally needed. They are frozen in liquid nitrogen and go into banks all over the country. Do you think that the healthy kidney you just saw would be better utilized decomposing in the ground, rather than give some dying citizen a long and happy life?'

165

'I'm not arguing. Just telling you how Charlie Vandeen feels. A man has a right to live or die his own way I've always believed.'

Grunting with the effort he bent and readied the machine to preserve the life of the dying Sheriff.

'N-no . . .' the Sheriff gasped. 'Take it away . . .'

'You're going to need this to save yourself, Charlie,' Doc said softly. 'This will keep you alive until we get you back to the hospital. We'll put a new pump in you then and you'll be good as new in a couple of weeks.'

'No,' the Sheriff said, louder now. 'Not to me you don't. I live and die with what God gave me. Do you think I could live with parts of someone else's body inside me. Why . . .' impotent tears filled his eyes ' . . . you might even be giving me my own little sister's heart.'

'No, not after all these years, Charlie. But I understand.' He waved away the man with the heart-lung machine. 'I'm just trying to help you, not make you do anything you think wrong.'

There was no answer. The Sheriff's eyes were open but he had stopped breathing. There, in those few seconds, he had passed that invisible dividing line. He was dead.

'He was a rough man but an honest one,' Doc Hoyland said softly. 'There have been a lot worse people in this world.' He closed the dead man's eyes and climbed painfully to his feet. 'I think we had better get back to work, doctor. There are a lot more people out there who need us.'

They had turned away when the ITB assistant called after them.

'Doctor, this man's not wearing a medallion.'

Doc Hoyland nodded. 'Not around his neck. He always said it might get torn off in an accident, must have told me a dozen times. Said that a sheriff always had his badge. You'll find the medallion soldered to the back of his badge.'

They were at the exit before the assistant called after them again. 'I'm sorry, doctor, but he doesn't seem to be wearing a badge. Are you sure about the medallion?'

'Of course I'm sure.' He turned shocked eyes to the ITB doctor who waited stolidly beside him. 'No – you can't! You know how he felt. I can send for his badge.'

'The law states that the medallion must be somewhere on the person.'

166

'I know the law, but you can't do this to him. Not Charlie. You can't . . .'

There were seconds of silence before the ITB doctor said: 'What do you think?'

Then, gently, he led the old doctor out.

If you would like a complete catalogue of
Quartet's publications please write to us at
27 Goodge Street, London W1P 1FD